STREET KNOWLEDGE PUBLISHING

Published by: **Street Knowledge Publishing**
Street Knowledge Publishing
P.O. Box 345
Wilmington, DE 19899

Copyright date: 2012
ISBN: 978-1-944151-04-1

Beyond Measure a novel by K. D. Harris
Edited by: Navimjan Services LLC
Cover design by: Street Knowledge Publishing Services
Formatted by: Krystol Diggs
Typed from handwriting to text by: Vanessa Cooper
Female model on cover:
Male model on cover:

All Street Knowledge Publishing titles are available at special quantity discounts for bulk purchases for sales promotion, fund-raising, educational, or institutional use and book clubs.

www.streetknowledgepublishing.com

Printed in Canada

Acknowledgments

God is so awesome! I can't believe that I am now releasing my third book. I give thanks to Bernard "Pooh John" Cornish the first person who ever laid eyes on any of my work and gave me the advice to never sleep on an opportunity. I thank you for believing in me before the world even knew there was a K.D Harris. Much love to Team K.D: Shanna, Tina, and C'Mor My Kreative Mind Foundation partners Alfred and Campbell.

To my brother John Coleman and his family I thank you all for the support. My babies Tryniti and Raevyn, J. Hall, Gina, Grandma Sheila, Uncle Donald & Aunt Sandy, My mom Barbara, Aunt Jackie, Cousin Sheena, Cousin Shelly, Bianca, Cousin Lisa Keep ya head up! My lil cousins Aniah and Mariyah Hall, Jaedyn and Nyaire Allen, Pat, and MooMoo, Carmelo, Donneshia my God children Kani and Breyon, my extended family nieces Nyia, Alysia and Brianna Lloyd always follow your dreams and be true to yourself.

To all of my supporters from my hometown Newark, Delaware. Cage 1, Brookmont Farms, Fettyville Music, Cousin Pizzle, Ms. Kiki, Shay, Robert and Diane Williams, Meka, Kish, Ronnie, Pre, lil Darren,(for help carrying my books…smile) and of course Robert Williams III, Aaron, Monique, Montwaine Lake, Cecelia, Alonzo "Littlez" Roberts and family. Cheryl Lyn Rodgers, Toya Russell, and Lashele Jones-Evans My girls since Gauger Middle. R.I.P A.J Chandler you are truly missed, Ms. Janet(mom) thank you for all you have done I appreciate you, Sheila and Todriana, Dante Feenix, Logan Herring, horizon books, Junnita Jackson, Julia Press Simmons, Kina Young, Paul Flowers of Sunlight books and Media. The Delaware Black Awards, 9th Street Book Shop, VJ Gotastory, Redeeming Grace World Wide Ministry, I know a few of yall still hold me up in prayer. To all of those who support me by buying my novels. I thank you and much love to you.

Last but not least Mrs. Michele A. Cameron - Fletcher, Thank you so much for believing in me 100%. I appreciate you.

Enjoy,
K.D.

www.facebook.com/kdharris·www.twitter.com/kdharris· www.kdharris.com

Dedication

Katchan Danee Reid
Without you there wouldn't be a K.D

The Beginning...

Usually on Saturday nights, I would spend my time watching the Sci-Fi channel's reruns of the 80's show. That's incredibly exciting right? Well things were about to change....

My life had been slowly diminishing for the last three years. Most people on the outside looking in would have loved to have be in my shoes. I had what some would consider a promising career as a psychologist in the Dual Diagnosis area at one of the nation's best Behavioral Health Centers. Not to mention my position as an *assistant* to the prestigious Dr. Gregory Hayward, who happens to be the best African American psychiatrist on the east coast.

Sounds pretty good, right?

Wrong.

My social life was on empty. How would you feel being in your early 30's with no husband, no kids, and no family, not even a distant cousin to share all of your accomplishments with? I don't even have any real close friends, unless you count a few of my halfway sane patients. I know you're probably thinking, *why don't you just try to go out and meet friends.*

My answer to that...it's not possible.

Not that I don't want to go out and have a good time. My career, or should I say the "Good Doctor" consumes all of my time. I'm always on call, Sunday through Saturday, 24 hours a day. Half the time I would just stay in my office, or sleep in one of the rooms at the hospital.

So you say, why not just find another career?

I can't because this is my life. It's what actually keeps me going. I love helping people, but here lately I feel that I have needed help myself. I have been feeling urges, unexplainable urges to do something.

What?

I have no idea. I feel like I have another part of me hidden somewhere that's dying to breakout.

Scary right?

I'm starting to sound like one of my patients. That's why sometimes I feel like ending it all. It's not like anyone would miss me anyway, especially Dr. Hayward. He treats me like I'm not even human half the time. That's one reason I never understood why he chose me for the job. There were others who I thought had more experience and deserved the position. For some reason or another he felt I was the one for the job.

Humph...some job.

I looked at the opportunity as a great accomplishment *at first*, but that soon changed. I hadn't been at the hospital two years, and I was getting a prominent position. There were candidates with more experience and had worked with Dr. Hayward for years, and for some reason they didn't even stand a chance at getting it.

Like my co-worker Karyn for instance; she worked closely with him and he treated her like *gold.* I was sure she was the one who would get the promotion. I remember us sitting in the break room having a cappuccino. Karyn perched her thin lips as she took sips of her French Vanilla cappuccino from the styrofoam cup. She leaned over across the small wooden table and whispered.

"Guess what!" Her eyes had a sparkle like a kid who just found their hidden x-mas gifts in the closet. "Gregory informed me this morning that he is announcing his decision about the assistant position this Friday at the treatment team meeting. By the way he was speaking he basically let me know I was getting the spot. I am so excited!" She was overjoyed.

She looked around to see if anyone was listening and whispered, "Don't worry Sasha, I won't forget about you, I'll put in a good word for you, maybe he'll let you come work under me."

I smiled weakly and nervously gave her a nod. I avoided direct eye contact with her due to the guilt I was feeling. I felt bad for her.

See, I also had a similar conversation with Gregory and our chat didn't lead me to believe she was getting the spot. In fact he told me I had the position. I was shocked of course but excited at the same time.

I felt false-hearted while celebrating her fictitious promotion. However, I didn't have the courage to shoot her dreams down, so I decided not to break the news. She would find out soon enough.

On Friday our team meeting was cancelled so there was no big announcement. However, she did receive her letter of denial. You would have thought her mother died the way she performed in that office. There was plenty of yelling, cursing, snot, and tears that morning. She stormed into Dr. Hayward's office for an explanation. Of course when she found out I was basically handed the job. She was hot and actually stopped speaking to me. If she knew what I was soon to find out she would be thanking the Heavens she didn't get it.

This is my story....

Chapter 1

After working an exhausting 16 hour shift at the Wilmington Site of the Christiana Medical Center, I was finally home. I swear it must have been a full moon last night. The patients were in an uproar; we had so many incidents that we had to call in help from hospital security.

Usually, I worked with the dual diagnosis crowd; you know the bi-polar, chemical dependents, anti- socials, basically the drug rehab clique.

Tonight they had me with the heavy hitters, the *D.I.D's*, Sociopaths, or should I say the APD's, those with anti-personality disorders. They were a trip and a half. You really had to be on your toes working with them. If you weren't careful they could have you falling right in their trap; they were both cunning and charming. A complete oxymoron but that described them perfectly.

The funny thing is we have so many people in our prison systems with these same characteristics that aren't diagnosed. If they had the proper diagnosis and treatment maybe we wouldn't have so many repeat offenders. Which is why my motto is "rehabilitation not imprisonation", if that's even a word. Hey if Mary can make up 'hateration', I'm good. But what do I know; I'm just a licensed therapist whose thoughts really didn't matter. They were Dr. Hayward's specialty.

I had a hold on things but I wasn't too familiar with my surroundings. I only worked at this facility when needed. Today was supposed to be my day off, but Dr. Hayward volunteered my services and sent me to help out.

I usually enjoyed going to Wilmington, because the Market Street Mall was just around the corner. I loved walking around the area enjoying the fresh air and doing a little cultural and tax free shopping. I just didn't like the drive; Rt. 202 is a mess with all the construction. I didn't understand why he just wouldn't send Karyn, or why he didn't go himself. They both lived in Delaware less than twenty minutes away from the Hospital. I however lived in Media, Pennsylvania just outside of West Chester where our main offices were located.

Finally home, I noticed a faint odor coming from my family room or home office area. The house was pitch black. I felt along the walls to find the light switch, and almost tripped over something. As I was falling my fingers found the switch flicking the lights on. Good thing too, because I almost hit my head on the 10lb dumbbell, that was lying on my wood floors. I managed to catch my balance by grabbing on to the bookshelf.

I really need to clean my house.

I moved the dumbbell to the top shelf with the other one, and made a mental note to take them back to the basement where they belonged.

"Oh my," I gasped as I held my hand covering my nose and mouth. The mystery was now over. I hurried over to my desk to remove the week old pasta, which had now grown green fur and a set of eye balls. I dumped the horrid smelling aged meal down the garbage disposal. I opened the cabinet under the sink where I kept my cleaning supplies and grabbed a can of Lysol antibacterial air freshener.

As I was making my way to my office to clear the air, my cell phone began to ring. *Who the hell is that* I thought. I looked at my pink Swarovski crystal embedded Dooney and Bourke watch and noticed it was a little after 10p.m. I picked up the phone and soon found out it was Dr. Hayward. I sighed.

What could he possibly want this late? I wanted to ignore him, but I knew he wouldn't give up until I answered the call.

"Ms. Jones, you need to report to the office, immediately." He didn't even give me a chance to greet him. I looked at the clock again and then looked at the phone in disgust.

Didn't he know I just worked a million hours and now he wants me to travel another 25 minutes to the office? I couldn't do this; he was over stepping his boundaries.

"Dr. Hayward, could we hold this off until the morning, I just got in from Delaware and I'm really tired-" Right in the middle of my sentence he cuts me off.

"Ms. Jones I didn't ask you about the hours you put in, let me remind you, you are in the helping profession, so you are an essential employee, meaning you are on call whenever I need you to be available, so I'm telling you as your superior that you need to get to this office immediately."

Click.

I stood there speechless holding the phone with tears in my eyes. I was so tired. I just wanted to relax and watch a little TV. I hung up the phone placed it in my purse then sat on the edge of my couch in disbelief.

Out of all the other therapist he had on staff, why would he decide to call me.

For a split second I thought about calling him back to tell him I quit. It's not like I didn't have a few dollars saved. It wouldn't be hard for me to get another job. Then reality hit. Who was I kidding, Dr. Hayward could have me black balled if I tried to leave him on bad terms.

I shook my head feeling defeated, and made my way up stairs. Standing in front of my whirlpool tub, I sighed deeply. I began to undress in defiance; I deserved a little relaxation and I was going to get it. He would just have to wait. I deserved some time to myself. I turned on the jets and added lavender bath oil while the water ran until it was nice and steaming hot.

As I eased myself down into the refreshing water I admired the aquamarine and sea foam green décor and closed my eyes. I loved the islands; at the rate I was going, I didn't know when I'd be able to take a vacation so I made my bathroom my getaway where I could always revisit them in my mind.

I stood in my wall length mirror as I dressed. I threw on a pair of black leggings and a lavender v-neck banded shirt. I knew it wasn't the proper attire and maybe even a little revealing. But I didn't care, I wasn't on the clock. I brushed my hair into a tight ponytail and slipped on my black ballerina flats. I looked in the mirror to make sure I was together. Thank God I did because I had forgotten to put them 38DD's in a bra. I then examined my face; I hated my complexion. I had an odd color almost copper like and it always seemed as if I was overly tanned. The only asset on my face was my green eyes. At least that's what I thought. Everyone always complemented me on my smile.

I was what they would call “cute”, but a little on the chubby side. I used to call them curves, but lately I had got so caught up in work I had no time to keep myself up the way I wanted. I felt myself getting depressed and quickly turned away.

Jogging down the stairs, I turned on the alarm and locked up the house. I looked at the clock when I got in the car and it was now 11:20. It's a wonder that Dr. Hayward didn't call me back. He was one of those types when he said jump, your reply better be “how high?” He was tough, but I had to admit he was very attractive.

Tall.

Dark.

Handsome...you know what every girl dreams about. I remember when he first hired me at the hospital. He was very direct about how he ran things and how the patients were our first priority. He barely had eye contact with me, and seemed to be talking at me more than talking to me. At that point, I decided to make sure I stayed on point and out of his way. But that didn't work. It seemed like he was constantly in my face about things that went wrong there.

I always wondered what he was like at home, and how his wife could tolerate him. Well scratch that, I know how she tolerated him. Again, the man was beautiful. God-like with a strong presence that makes you melt; until he opens his mouth that is. I laughed to myself.

I wonder if they even had sex, and what it would be like. Would he give direct orders in his lifeless tone? Or, would he just lay there and make her do all the work, and then complain about it. I burst out in uncontrollable laughter picturing him doing just that. I pulled into my parking spot, turned to my left and Dr. Hayward was standing there with a blank look on his face.

My smile dropped. I could not believe he was actually outside waiting. It was not that serious. When I got out the car he began to complain immediately.

"I thought I told you to come here as soon as possible. It's been over an hour since we spoke. You know how I feel about insubordination, Ms. Jones." He was pissed as usual.

He turned around and started walking towards the building. I followed behind him with my head down, not wanting him to see the smirk on my face.

As we were walking in I noticed how nice his butt was. To my surprise he had on a pair of True Religion jeans with a matching button up top. I couldn't believe it. I had to give it to him he had a little style going on.

Wait a minute what is wrong with me.

I had to check myself, I don't know what had gotten into me, but I knew I had no business checking my boss out. When we entered the building, I started towards the elevator so I could escape him and get myself together.

"Where are you going Ms. Jones? I told you I needed you in my office."

Against my own will I immediately stopped in my tracks and followed him to his office quietly. We reached his office and he unlocked the heavy steel door. I decided to hurry and plead my case before he tore into me.

"Dr. Hayward, I had to shower, I had a long day and…" I just stopped in the middle of my sentence as a shudder went up my spine. An odd feeling came over me suddenly. I felt nauseas and nervous, like something was about to happen. All of my questions were about to be answered, when I walked completely through his office door. The bizarre feeling became more intense, when I noticed him lock his door.

An out of the ordinary noise caught my attention. I directed my eyes to the area where he would conduct his therapy sessions. My mouth dropped to the floor. Were my eyes deceiving me or was there a stark naked man pleasing himself. I was stunned and embarrassed. I turned to Dr. Hayward for an explanation.

"Oh…my God," I half whispered. I had to get the hell out of there quick. I tried to rush past him but he grabbed me.
Without saying a word he put his finger up to my lips, signaling for me to be quiet. He began to smile, something that I had never seen him do. It was a warm but sexy smile.

I felt myself beginning to get a little bothered. A feeling that I hadn't felt in a long time was starting to surface.

"Ms. Jones, how about you take a seat over there?" He said calmly pointing to a seat on the couch next to the naked chocolate brother.

Of course I was hesitant, but there was something else taking over my logical thinking. "Uhh, Dr. Hayward, I don't…I'm not sure, what's going on…."

Dr. Hayward signaled for me to be quiet again. I tried not to look at the man but I couldn't help myself. The man resembled Dr. Hayward.

"Ms. Jones this is my brother Lorenz."

Brother? This was bad, and I had to get out of there and fast.

"Dr. Hayward, I have to go this is not right, I don't know what you're trying to do, but I'm not like that I'm not that kind of…."

"Sasha, calm down sweetie," He said caressing my shoulders. "You need to lighten up and enjoy yourself. I know there's more to you. Don't tell me you're all work and no play."

Lighten up? I couldn't believe what I was hearing. Mr. I - gotta- stickup-my-ass was telling me to lighten up. I began to laugh out of confusion. I moved away from him and placed my hand on my left hip.

"Are you serious, as much hell as you give me you got the nerve to tell me to lighten up?" I was infuriated. How dare he think I was some cheap whore. At this point I didn't care what I said. I looked back at the man on the couch who seemed to not be paying us any mind. He continued to massage himself. My heart was racing with both anger and excitement. I tried not to watch the show, but I couldn't help it. He was definitely working with something special, and I had to admit it happened to look very good from where I was standing.

Smooth… Flawless… Thick.

Very appetizing.

Dr. Hayward stood up and walked around me. He then put his hands on my side and slowly moved them around to my breasts.

I began to stutter, "You need to stop, I'm not a whore, this is unethical." I tried to stand my ground but his touch sent sensual electric impulses through my body. I hadn't felt like that in years. He then slid one of his hands under my shirt and began to squeeze my breasts and pinch my now erect nipples. I trembled from the excruciating pleasure.

He whispered in my ear seductively. "Relax, and just let this flow…remove your clothes so I can see how beautiful you are."

In my mind I knew this was wrong, but my body was yelling for it. I hesitated for a moment. He noticed my resistance and slid his masculine hands inside my pants and began to slowly lower them. Against my better judgment I closed my eyes and let him have his way. Deep down in my heart I had longed for this man's attention, just didn't expect for it to come in this manner. Never in a million years would I have imagined myself standing there half naked in the middle of his office. I heard movement coming from the opposite direction. I no longer felt Dr. Hayward's touch, but I felt someone leading me towards the couch.

When I opened my eyes it was the brother. He reminded me of Morris Chestnut, with his deep chocolate complexion, and neatly trimmed beard. He laid me down on the couch and began to explore my body with his mouth. It felt so good.

"Let me taste you." His voice was as smooth and suave as his movements.

He gently spread my legs and placed his head between them. I felt the tip of his nose rub against my lips and clitoris. I quivered and my heart rate increased. I jumped when I felt his fingers plunge into my abyss followed by his thick tongue. I moaned deeply as he made love to me with his mouth as he took in the essence of my love juices.

I was in total bliss.

He lifted my thick legs up and placed them on his shoulders. I braced myself for what was about to take place. It had been three years since I had a man enter me. He licked his thick lips as he gazed at me with his bedroom eyes. He had me hypnotized as I stared dreamily into them.

Then it happened, he thrust his thickness into me without warning. I tried to contain myself but I couldn't, deep moans of passion escaped from my mouth. He swiveled his hips in a rhythm that only he could hear as he pounded me. I was so into it that I had forgotten all about Dr. Hayward. I turned my head to look for him and he was sitting in his chair stroking his dick. It was too late to be in embarrassed or to turn back the hands of time. I was enjoying myself and the damage was already done. I was open and I loved every bit of it.

Chapter 2

The next morning, I laid in the bed in total confusion. The events that took place the night before had changed my life and I was afraid of what that would mean for me. After the sexcapade was over; Dr. Hayward decided to inform me that not only was Lorenz his brother but my new intern. I felt like crap.
I wanted to resign on the spot; I began to question my integrity.

I couldn't believe what I participated in. That was not the person I was...or was it?

At this point I wasn't sure if I knew who I was. I felt a sense of freedom.

Shame…

Satisfaction!

I hugged my pillow tightly and bit down on my lip as I thought about what happened again. Tears escaped the corners of my eyes. I didn't know if they were tears of joy, fear, or disappointment.

I was happy because Dr. Hayward finally showed me some attention. However, I was afraid to face him today after my performance last night. How would he treat me now that he had something so morally wrong over my head? I sat up. Feeling frustrated I threw my pillow.

"Damn, Sash you fucked up! You are a professional." I reminded myself out loud.

How could I have screwed my boss's brother, who just happens to be my new intern? My sobs began to turn into soft laughter when I saw the deranged look on my face in the mirror. I was convinced; I am turning into one of my patients. I sat up and grabbed a Kleenex off my nightstand to wipe my face. I looked at the clock and noticed the time, 9:00 a.m. I was late.

Oh shit, I jumped up and showered quickly. I threw on a soft pink sweater and a gray pencil skirt with knee boots. I applied some lip gloss and sprayed on a little Allure perfume, grabbed my file bag, and ran out the door.

On my drive to the hospital, visions of the exploit from the night before filled my head. A few times I found myself getting lost in my thoughts, which caused me to swerve on the highway. After a few horns and curses from my fellow drivers, I got myself together.

I entered the building and couldn't help but to think everyone knew what happened. It seemed as if everyone was staring at me. I knew it was all in my mind. I entered the elevator and pushed five. As the door opened, I looked around before I got off. I was sure Dr. Hayward would be waiting for me, but he wasn't there. As I opened the door to my office, Lorenz was sitting there waiting for me instead.

I was stunned.

I hesitated before walking to my chair. He stood up as I proceeded in and extended his hand.

A hand shake. Is he serious? Did he forget how he had his face buried between my legs just the night before?

I nodded my head in acknowledgement and sat down. It seemed like the walls were closing in on me. My breathing became shallow and suddenly it became stuffy. I had the notion that I was going to pass out. I took deep breaths trying to get myself together.

"Ms. Jones are you alright?" Concern was in his voice.
I looked at him surprisingly.

"Y-yes I'm fine. It's just a little hot in here."I pulled out a portable fan that I kept underneath my desk.

"Well let me properly introduce myself I'm Lorenz Hayward, as you know I will be your intern for the next several months."

His voice, baritone and mesmerizing; It was so smooth and calming with a medium flow like a melody from Kenny G.

"I really admire your working methods, and I am excited to have the opportunity to work with someone with your standards." He gave me a sly smile.

My work methods? I bet.

I couldn't help but blush, which showed off my dimples.

"I hope you don't mind me saying this, but you have a beautiful smile."

"Thank you...Mr. Hayward."

I have to get control of this conversation; If he keeps coming at me with compliments, we are going to be rolling around on this floor.

I pulled up a case file on my desk and began to focus on that. Hopefully he would catch my drift and excuse himself. Instead he decided to fill me in on his background; which was fine with me. I learned he graduated from Penn State and was now in the University of Maryland's Doctorate program. Turns out that Lorenz was quite a talker, a whole hour had passed, and that's when I realized that I hadn't heard from Dr. Hayward.

"Is Dr. Hayward here today? I usually get a call from him by now."

"Oh you didn't know, this weekend is his 11th wedding anniversary, he and Camille are going to the islands."

I immediately felt sick. I forgot about poor Mrs. Hayward. I wondered how she would feel if she knew what her husband was into. I looked in my desk for an Excedrin as I felt a major headache coming on.

"Mr. Hayward, could you please excuse me I have a few charts that I really need to complete. You can go to B-Wing and get familiar with some of our patients personally, or you can just study their charts, it's totally up to you." I didn't mean to sound harsh, but I had a lot to think about.

He wore a saddened expression on his face as he walked out the door. I admired his frame from my desk. He was tall, about 6'3, milk chocolate skin, with side burns and deep dimples. His body was thick with an athletic build. He must have felt me gazing as he walked out the door, because he turned around and smiled. That's when my mind started to wonder back to the night before.

My pussy started to twitch, and I felt myself getting wet. I tried to concentrate on a case file to ignore the feeling, but it wouldn't go away. The twitching between my legs became more intense. I had to get out of there. I called my secretary and asked her to block out all appointments. I was in no shape to see anyone to discuss their issues. I was having my own at the time, and it needed to be handled.

I went into my closet and grabbed a pillow. I locked my office door and pulled my chair away from my desk. I took off my skirt and lay on my stomach on the floor. I slipped my fingers inside my panties, crossed my legs, and began rubbing my clit and squeezing my thighs together. I held onto the pillow and went into a deep erotic trance. I imagined the pillow was Lorenz and he was fucking the hell out of my pussy.

In my dream he had me bent over my desk ramming his thickness all inside of me, while smacking my big round ass. I squeezed my thighs harder and started to grind my hips. I went back into my dream: Lorenz was still fucking me from behind pushing my head onto the papers on my desk. It seemed so real that it felt as if I could feel his balls hitting my wet pussy.

I squeezed my thighs tighter.

I was now making small whimpering noises and actually talking to the pillow as if it were him. I was no longer playing with my clit. I was now focused on my dream. I clawed at the pillow and grinded the floor while squeezing my walls until I felt a pulsating sensation. I reached my orgasm. My heart was beating heavily, and my juices soaked my panties. I laid there so I could catch my breath. My body was satisfied. I got up off the floor, grabbed a new pair of panties I had in my office for moments like these and went to the bathroom to freshen up.

Chapter 3

Two weeks had gone past since my episode with my boss and his brother, *my intern*. Dr. Hayward had returned back to work from his vacation. He was back to his self righteous, disgruntled self. I was starting to wonder if I was tripping, and imagined the whole encounter. Lorenz changed when his brother came back. The sweet comments stopped, he was acting as if I didn't exist. Neither one of them expressed any emotion toward me, just straight faced and clinical about everything.

The only thing I had left was a memory and my private sessions with my pillow under my desk in my office. Maybe it was for the best. That just reminded me, I needed to go and pick up some new panties. I decided to head over to Granite Run Mall. I knew Lane Bryant was still open. It was 8p.m. and I was in my office finishing a report. I shut down my computer, and rose from my desk, grabbed my jacket and turned the knob to leave out. When I pulled the door open Dr. Hayward was there. I froze, this was the first time we were alone since the night in his office.

"Good evening Dr. Hayward, umm I was just leaving I…I have a few errands to run." I was nervous and it showed.

He just stood in front of the door not budging. I felt like a little girl who was sneaking out and was caught by her imperious father. I could feel my blood running rapidly through my veins.

I told him again with a pleading voice, "Dr. Hayward, I

have errands to run, and I *really* need to go."

I got bold and tried to gently push pass him. He was unmovable like a boulder. He wore a blank expression on his face as he watched me. I tried not to have direct eye contact with; I was afraid of what was about to transpire.

Silence surrounded us.

I had no room for escape. I couldn't cry out for help, everyone had already left for the evening. Besides what good would that do it's not like he was doing anything to hurt me. He was just freaking me out by standing there showing no signs of any emotions. Almost as if he was in a daze.

Out of nowhere he quietly moved away from the door; not taking his eyes off me as I hurried past him down the hall. Just before I hit the elevators I heard him say.

"Sasha, look in your jacket pocket."

I patted both pockets of my peacoat and felt something in the one on the left. I pulled out a Hilton Key Card. I was confused. I looked in his direction for answers. He spoke again in an authoritative manner.

"You have 25 minutes to get there, no exceptions."

He shut the door to my office and walked in the opposite direction, not even giving me a chance to say anything. On the way to my car, I became instantly angry. I was going through a battle in my mind.

What the hell is going on? Sasha, what did you go and get yourself into?"

I started my car and sat for a moment contemplating if I should go or not. Part of me wanted to go, I couldn't lie to myself; I enjoyed my night with Lorenz. What I couldn't understand was why Lorenz just couldn't come to me himself and ask me out. The million dollar question was what was Dr. Hayward getting out of this? Was he just some freak that got off by watching his brother sex females? Curiosity was winning. I put the car in reverse and headed towards the airport. I had 20 minutes to get my ass to that Hilton and I did just that.

***

At 8:35, I was unlocking the door to room 336. I entered, looked around to see if he was there and I noticed I was alone. I noticed a note sitting on the table. I picked it up and read it.

Ms. Jones, I want you to shower, and then put on the outfit I have for you on the bed.

It had Dr. Hayward's signature. I threw the note back down.

What is this some sort of game?

I walked to the bedroom area, and on the bed was a gorgeous white silk nightgown. It was quite revealing, cut very low in the front and the back dropped. I checked the tag and noticed he had picked the right size.

Lucky guess.

I went to the bathroom to undress for my shower and saw that he even had my favorite fragrances and shower gels. The doctor had been doing research on me. For some reason I began to relax more.

Maybe this is not what I think it is.

I continued to remove my clothes and turned the water on. Once it was at the right temperature, I hopped in. I turned the shower head to massage mode and let the water beat down on my back. It felt so good beating down on me that I closed my eyes and started caressing my breasts. My nipples were enlarged and very hard. I looked down and my breasts looked like two ripe cantaloupes. I started to squeeze them harder. I felt tingling between my thighs and I was about to handle that but I heard a door close. I washed the soap off and quickly dried off and lotion myself.

I looked around for the gown, but had left it on the bed. I tried to cover up with the towel, but it didn't go all the way around me. I was pissed. I started to curse out the Hilton about their itty bitty towels, but instead covered up as much as I could and made my way out.

When I opened the door, to my surprise, Dr. Hayward stood before me. The uneasy feeling was back. He went over to the bar and poured himself a glass of Merlot. He then made his way over to the bed and patted it for me to sit beside him.

"Uhh...could you give me a minute? I just needed to grab

this…." I quickly grabbed the gown from the bed.

He gently grabbed my arm. He took off his glasses and sat them on the night stand. He had this blank look on his face staring me dead in my eyes. It seemed as if he were looking through me. He stood in front of me and began to unbuckle his pants. He took off his belt.

"Ms. Jones I want you to lay on your stomach with your hands behind your back."

I sat there for a moment before I moved. I took a look at him holding that thick leather belt and fear set in. I measured my distance from the front door, but decided against trying to escape. I was naked and I didn't want to cause a scene running naked through the hallway. I decided I'd better follow his directions. I slowly spread across the bed on my stomach. My body began to tremble in terror of the unknown. I heard him unzipping his pants. I turned my head over to the mirror and saw Dr. Hayward undressing. For a man of his age, his body wasn't bad. He was in shape. I saw him reach for both my arms. He gently pulled them behind me putting both of my wrists together. He was tying them with the belt.

I whimpered "*ouch*", as he was doing it. "Please Dr. Hayward…I can't do this."

He ignored me.

Once my hands were secure, he rolled me on my back. He grabbed three pillows and positioned them under my head in an elevated position. He moved up further towards my face while he was on his knees. I held my breath not sure of what he was about to do. He took his manhood, which was pretty thick, I mean really thick; like a small wrist, and began to rub it in between my breasts. He was stroking between them in a slow, steady motion. My breathing became rapid but this was not from anxiety I was being turned on.

He just squeezed my breast firmly and picked up the pace. I was getting excited, my walls were pulsating crying out for attention, but he didn't seem interested. I on the other hand, had an uncontrollable urge to feel him inside of me. I bit down on my lip trying to contain myself. My hands were tied so I couldn't touch myself. He pumped harder and faster between them. He pinched my nipples and grabbed my tits. I had begun to scream because it was torturing me.

My pussy was throbbing and jumping so badly, I wanted him to just let my hands free. I couldn't even squeeze my thighs. I tried to move around to calm it, but that didn't help. I looked at Dr. Hayward, my eyes pleading for him to fuck me, but he continued to stroke between my breasts. This was so intense. I wanted to cry, my body was burning; I needed to feel him in me. The doctor was in control, like always. My arms were hurting from all the weight being on them, but that was in the back of my mind. I don't know what his intentions were but he was definitely bringing out another side of me I didn't know existed.

He was about to cum; He took his swollen dick and crammed it down my throat. As soon as it was in my mouth, he filled my cheeks with hot creamy liquid. I started to gag, but he didn't pull out. He lifted my head up.

"Swallow" he ordered.

Afterwards, he untied my hands, kissed me on the forehead, and left. When I heard the door shut I sat up completely in the bed. I placed my hand on the nightstand, but sharp pains shot through my wrists. I looked at my wrists and they were red and swollen. I guess the weight and being in that position so long took a toll on them. I looked down at my breasts and you could see evidence of the abuse Dr. Hayward inflicted. I had bruises from the tugging, and extreme squeezing. He was not a gentle lover at all. He was very brutal physically and emotionally.
But I can't complain because I let this happen. Just as I was examining my bruises, my cell phone rang. I slowly got off the bed and made my way across the room to answer it. As I opened it to say hello, the room door opened. I paused and went to see who came in and the familiar voice on the phone said, "Don't you tell anyone I was there tonight! I mean no one!" Then I heard a dial tone.

It was Dr. Hayward on the phone. I looked at the phone in confusion and yelled out, "WHO IS IN THIS ROOM?"

I grabbed my jacket that was lying on the chair to cover up.

Then the bedroom doors opened and Lorenz walked in. I pulled my jacket tighter around me.

"What are you doing here?"

He grinned as he sized me up like a wolf who was about to devour his prey, "Oh you want to play games?"

His demeanor was different, slightly cocky but in a sarcastic way. He went over to the bed and started taking his clothes off.

"Mr. Hayward, what are you doing?" I was confused.

What type of game are they playing?

He snickered.

"Mr. Hayward."

He gave me a questioning look as he looked on the floor and found the night gown.

"Easy access the way I like it...."

He headed in my direction with a wild look on his face like he was about to attack me. I stood still. My mind was saying run but I couldn't. I was in a sexual trance; there was something about him that brought out another side of me. The closer he came to me the heavier my breathing became. I was anxious to see what was in store.

His body was magnificent physically fit but thick. He was muscular in all the right places, and that muscle dangling between his legs would really satisfy my craving for dick.

We were face to face.

"I've been waiting for this. I thought you would have asked for this dick sooner. When I received your e-mail this afternoon, I couldn't wait to get to you."

I snapped out of it.

"E-mail, what e-mail? I didn't send an email." I could feel his minty breath over my lips.

"Ok...I'll play the game with you. I know you want to be discreet. I read it. I'll do everything that you asked." He ripped the jacket from around my body and grabbed me violently.

I was startled, but I went along with it. I was turned on. He squeezed my bruised breast, I tensed up from pain. My actions caused him to examine them.

"Damn, I guess you really do like it rough...."

He stuffed my nipple in his mouth and began to bite down hard. I covered my mouth so the screams couldn't escape. He picked me up and tossed me on the bed.

"So you like it rough…huh bitch?" He had a sinister grin on his face.

I got offended.

"Bitch? You're out of line I don't know what type of game you…." I stopped myself. I remembered the warning that I had just received from his brother. I took a deep breath. "Lorenz, I need you to leave…."

He continued to stand over top of me with his hard dick dangling. I had to get myself together and stop this charade something was not right, and I had to stop it before I lost myself completely. I jumped up from the bed attempting to escape to the bathroom.

He caught me grabbing me tightly in his arms, "Where are you going?" He ran his hands down my arm until he reached my wrist. He loosened his grip and gently held my hand in his.

"Sasha, what happened?" His whole character changed instantly. He examined my wrist, "Does this hurt?" he pressed on it gently. I pulled back. Maybe he didn't really know what was going on. I couldn't be too sure. He was a psychologist and just like our patients we knew how to play the game of manipulation.

I went to the bathroom and brought out two cold rags he wrapped them around both of my wrist and led me to the bed. He laid down and gently pulled me to him and held me. We shared no words, he just held me until we both fell asleep.

Chapter 4

The next morning I was enjoying the ride of my life. His fingers dug deeply into my ass cheeks as I rocked back and forth on his face. He moved his arms to my thighs and pressed down firmly taking me deeper. If he kept this up his tongue would be tickling my ovaries. He was inhaling my pussy. I felt myself let loose several times until I fell back from exhaustion.

"Oh no, you're not getting off that easy," he teased.

He grabbed me by my hips and sat me on his dick. All 11 inches went into me. It felt like he knocked something out of place. He continued to brutalize my pussy until it was numb. I didn't think that was possible.

I was high off his dick.

It never crossed my mind that we should be using a condom. Not even when I felt his hot juices flow inside me. I rolled off his dick into his arms. I thought he was going to be like his brother and leave, but he didn't. He whispered in my ear, "Did you enjoy yourself? Did I fulfill your fantasy?"

I nodded my head.

I had no idea what he was talking about. I was worn out.

I believe this is the most excitement I have had in my whole life.

Bizarre? Yes.

However the experience was exciting. A feeling of extreme happiness overcame me.

As he lay next to me I studied his facial features. He had nice full lips, defined cheek bones, and beautiful brown eyes. I noticed how he really resembled Dr. Hayward. He was just a younger version.

The phone call came back to my mind. It made me wonder about this situation.

Did Dr. Hayward know he was coming? And why did he want to keep it a secret?

Then it dawned on me.

Dr. Hayward sent the e-mail! What type of game was he playing? What made him think that I wanted to be treated this way?

Although I didn't agree with the games Dr. Hayward was playing. I had to admit I was starting to enjoy this attention. It still boggled me that I didn't know the reasoning behind all of this.

Why now?

A sickening feeling came over me.

What if he's using me as one of his researches?

I removed myself from Lorenz's embrace and jumped out of the bed. He didn't budge. I guess he was worn out too. I grabbed my clothes and threw them on. I looked back at him while he slept. He looked so innocent. I wonder if he had any idea of his brother's plans. I walked over to the bed to looked at him one more time. I didn't want to leave. My body was aching, but I could have gone another round with him. I shook my head and turned to walk away.

I felt a sudden tug at my waist. He was behind me pulling me closer to him. I could feel that lovely third leg of his against my ass.

"Why are you leaving so fast? It's your day off, you don't have to work." He began to massage my back. I was ready to melt again. I had to stand my ground. I turned around to face him.

"I have to run errands today. I need to get started early," I lied.

I think he believed me because he released his grasp. He gently grabbed my face and gave me a wet passionate kiss, gently sucking my lips and tongue. I had to make a move because I could feel myself getting lost again. I moved back.

"Can I see you tonight?"

I didn't even think twice about my answer, "Sure, that would be nice. I'll prepare dinner for us. Do you like Italian?

"Yes, that's one of my favorite types of food."

There was that breath taking smile again. I wanted to stay in his presence forever. That just wasn't possible because I had too many unanswered questions. I was on my way to the hospital to talk to Dr. Hayward. I refused to be anyone's lab rat.

***

Dr. Hayward was sitting at his desk with his hands folded like he was waiting for me. I hated how he somehow knew everything. I closed the door behind me, and he smiled.

I glared at him.

"Dr. Hayward, What the hell is going on? What was last night about? I marched over to him and yelled in a hush tone.
Look at what you did to me!" I pulled up my sweater and exposed my breasts.

They were covered in red blotches that would soon turn to purple and blue bruises. "Look what you did!" I felt tears starting to fall. "Why are you doing this to me?"

I pulled my sweater back down and sat on his couch. Which were the couches where Lorenz and I first had our encounter, I began to sob uncontrollably.

Dr. Hayward finally spoke, "Sasha, I didn't do anything to you. You wanted this." I lifted my head up, astounded by what he just said.

"I wanted this? Are you serious?" I shook my head in disgust.

He sat on the couch next to me. He began to stroke the back of my neck. "Relax…This is what you want. Isn't this what you want Sasha?"

I shook my head no.

"Yes...you do want this Sasha."

"Dr. Hayward, I don't! I am confused. I don't understand

this, and why did you send that email?" He ignored my question and continued to massage my neck.

"Sasha, you need a vacation. I'm sending you away tonight."

I removed his hands from my neck although the massage was feeling lovely.

"I am *your* boss and you *are* going away for a few days. You are going to Florida, I have a conference there I have to attend, and you'll be my private guest. You will leave tonight at 11p.m. from the Philadelphia Airport. I will send a car to come and get you. Pack lightly; I will supply all your needs. Don't worry about any money. I will meet you there Monday." He walked over to his desk and handed me a packet.

"This packet has all of the accommodation details. All the information you need is inside." He walked to the door to show me out.

"This is between you and I. No one is to know where you are going." He nudged me out of his office and shut the door.

I stood there baffled.

I left feeling defeated and more confused than when I went in. He still didn't give me any answers. I drove in deep thought.

Did I really want all this? Did I somehow bring this all on myself? Maybe he is right.

I was losing myself rapidly. I didn't even know who I was becoming and it was scaring me. Maybe I do want this. I could have reported him for sexual harassment when it first started. I didn't. I had a choice in all of this.

When I pulled into my driveway, I noticed a package in my doorway so I grabbed it as I was going in. Reading the label, it was a box of flowers. I opened the box and there were twelve long stem white roses, with one red. I read the card and it was from Lorenz. It read:

For you 'Honey Brown'.

I smiled to myself. Interrupted by my doorbell ringing, I went to the door and an oversized Pooh Bear with a honey jar was on my doorstep.

I carried both the flowers and the bear upstairs and sat them on the bed. I ran my bath water as I thought about Lorenz. I think he really may like me. He's a cutie and a great lover. But how could I establish anything real with him and I'm leaving with his brother tonight. I tried not to think about it. I was going to make tonight really special for him and me. Who knows, this may be our last time together.

Chapter 5

It was now 4p.m., only an hour before Lorenz was to show up. I decided not to serve dinner. My appetite was for something else and it wasn't Italian. I can't believe what has been happening, I felt like a new person. I felt free. I had to make an excuse to get him out of here no later than 7p.m. I didn't want him to see the car picking me up. I didn't want to run the risk of him asking questions that I just couldn't answer.

I called him around 2p.m. this afternoon. I sounded like an emotional wreck as I told him my non-existing sister was going through a crisis with her non-existing husband. So we would have to cut the evening short, because I had to fly to Atlanta tonight. You could hear the disappointment in his voice as he expressed his concern for the situation. We decided to make our date earlier. I felt bad when I hung up the phone. A liar was something I'd never been in the past, but I knew I would have to start getting used to it. I sighed and continued getting myself together.

I didn't want to get fully dressed since the clothes were coming off anyway. I also didn't want to come down in my mom-mom pj's. I didn't own any sexy evening wear, so I decided to be daring and wear nothing. I pulled a short white Terry Cloth robe from my closet and my house slippers. I knew it wasn't sexy but I doubt if he was interested in my attire. He just wanted to get in me and I didn't mind that at all.

I made sure I put my Allure on, a little nude lip-gloss, and ran my fingers through my hair. Thank God, I got the good stuff. I don't know what I'd do if I had to worry about relaxers and curling irons all the time.

My hair was naturally curly. My mother told me my father was from Panama, and that's where I get the good hair from. I never understood that because the Panamanian kids I went to school with had nappy hair. I had to laugh. I missed my mother: she would say and do the craziest things. As I looked in the mirror staring at my reflection, I never realized how much I looked like her. But my awe faded as disappointment fell over me; I wondered what she would think regarding what I was doing. I felt a lump forming in my throat and had to shake it off, no time for an emotional breakdown. I was on a mission.

I looked at the clock. I had 20 minutes before my company arrived. Next to the clock I noticed the package Dr. Hayward had given me. I just realized that I never opened it. I looked through it and it had everything he said, airline ticket, reservation codes, a VISA card, and two thousand dollars worth of American Express gift checks. Wow, I thought he sure is being nice. I picked up a computer printout that read Old Key West Resort.

What we're going to Disney?

I had to laugh, Dr. Hayward at Disney World. That didn't quite match up.

My thoughts were interrupted by the doorbell. He's here; I clapped my hands together like a little kid. I put the information back in the envelope, and set it on my bed. I had to get my composure together as I walked to the door. I stopped before answering to think how I would greet him. Should I be timid as always? Should I just jump on him and take what I wanted. This was fun. I decided to be the aggressor. I opened the door and pulled him in. I wrapped my arms around him and starting kissing his neck. I think I caught him off guard because he looked at me in shock.

I was embarrassed.

"Oh. I'm so sorry, I just thought...oh never mind." I walked over to my sofa. He followed me. He sat next to me and put his hands in mine.

"Sasha, I don't want you to think of me as just your fuck

buddy. I really admire you, inside and out."

Instant attitude set in. I didn't want to hear that, I wanted to fuck.

"I really admire you," he went on. "I know we didn't meet under the best circumstances. But I've watched you for years."

Watched me for years?

That night in Dr. Hayward's office was the first night I ever met him. He saw the puzzled look on my face. That's when he explained everything.

"See I had been to the hospital several times before. I never really had the chance to meet you personally, but from the first time I laid eyes on you I knew you were something special."

I felt my face get hot with embarrassment. I wasn't used to hearing a man talk like that about me. I can't believe I never noticed him in the past. Then again I was always buried in my work. He continued to confess his feelings for over 45 minutes. I thought to myself, I have to make a move before we have no more time left. I mean I was feeling everything he said and I was flattered he was showing me a softer side. It felt good to be wanted for more than sex; but at that moment, that's what I wanted...hot unadulterated sex!

I had had enough of the soft talk. I took matters into my own hands, literally. I kissed him on his lips gently and nibbled on his ear. I straddled myself on top of his lap and whispered in a sexy voice.

"I'm flattered that you like me, really I am and I want to show my appreciation."

I began kissing him on his neck seductively. I instructed him to take off his sweater. I kissed all over his bare chest. I loved his chest; he was so well cut. I nibbled and sucked his nipples alternating between the two. He started to quiver. I think I found his hot spot! I continued to get him aroused by rubbing his manhood that began to swell in my hands. When it was nice and firm, I dropped to my knees and attempted to deep throat him. I felt myself gag just a little, but I continued to give him some throat action. Using no hands, I worked my tongue along the bulging veins of his shaft. It must have been good to him, because he began to beg for me to take it deeper within my mouth, and I did.

I had so much saliva built up, that it was seeping out the corners of my mouth. He was really getting into it. He stood up and began to thrust my head towards him for me to take it even deeper. Tears started to form in my eyes. I was gagging so badly, I felt like I was going to vomit, but I had to hold back. His balls were slapping against my chin. It sounded like he was forcing himself deeper. My body began to jerk as if I was ready to hurl. Lorenz took that as a warning and bent me over the arm of the sofa.

Finally, I was going to feel that dick of his in me again. He ran his dick up the crack of my ass to tease me. Then he pushed his way deep inside my pussy. He did it with such force that I came immediately. He massaged my back as he slowly stroked my "girl" doggie style. I was in heaven. I moaned lightly as he squeezed my ass. He was really different tonight. He was very gentle and loving? He whispered sweet things to me.

"Sasha…you are so beautiful, and you feeeeel soooo good inside," he moaned.

I could have stayed in that position forever but reality hit, and I had a plane to catch. I started to tighten my walls around his pleasure tool.

"Sasha…ple…please stop I'm not ready to cum…He stammered.

I wasn't about to stop, I needed him to cum. I continued to tighten my muscles until he came. Again, I was filled with his love juices. He lay on top of me until his pole went completely limp. I watched the clock hoping he would hurry and get off me. After a few tender kisses to the neck, he finally slid out of my hole. Not giving him a chance to get comfortable, I scurried off the couch.

I took hold of his hand pulling him up and handed him his pants.

"I hate to do this, but I have to get ready to catch my flight."

He was upset; you could see it all in his face. He rose up and started to dress himself. I helped him button his shirt. He kissed me again.

"Sasha, I meant everything I said tonight." I nodded and handed him his sweater.

"We will talk about it when I get back, but I really have to get ready for my flight," I insisted.

He went to my wash room to freshen up. Once he was done I showed him to the door. He kissed me again. "Don't have me wait too long…call me to let me know you landed safely."

I was happy! I couldn't believe I was feeling this way.

He cares. He really cares about me!

I watched him as he pulled out of my driveway; I couldn't wait to get back to see him.

Chapter 6

I was on cloud nine. I couldn't believe what had occurred over the past several weeks. It seemed so unbelievable that I had a love interest; I had someone who was interested in me. He was successful, attractive, and he really liked *me* for who I am. Who would have thought after that Saturday's office situation, he could take me seriously.

On the shuttle bus that was taking me to Old Key West, I slept through the entire plane ride. Because we arrived so quickly, it seemed as if I was only flying for ten minutes. Even though it was 3 a.m., I thought about calling Lorenz, but knew it was too late. Instead, I called Dr. Hayward's voicemail and let him know that I had arrived and would call back in the morning.

As we approached the resort, I was quite impressed with the scenery. It reminded me of the Caribbean so I was thrilled. Beautiful palm trees, a huge golf course, boats that were docked, and a beautiful replica of a sand castle that turned into a water slide. It was beautiful at night and could only imagine how it would look during the day. I grabbed my bags to go check in.

The front desk clerk gave me a hard time. The woman looked to be about my age; she had fiery red hair and glowing green eyes. She wasn't friendly at all, and I had no idea why she wanted to pick an argument with me. She looked me up and down like I was trailer trash.

"You mean to tell me you don't have a key?" she sneered.

"No ma'am, I already explained to you the situation. I am

here on business, my boss just told me to check in, and everything would be fine," I was getting frustrated; I didn't realize this was a time share property.

"I find it hard to believe that Dr. Hayward would send you here without a key. Are you sure you're in the right place? You weren't supposed to be at the Day's Inn down the road or something?" She was being sarcastic.

I know she's not insinuating that I was some type of whore.

I wasn't going to deal with her any further; she was trying to start something. Why? I don't know but I refused to let her take me there. "I need to speak to a manager."

"Excuse me?"

That got her attention.

"Maybe you can't comprehend so I'm going to say it slowly. I…need …to... speak…with…your...manager." She rolled her eyes and turned around slowly dragging her feet.

Moments later she returned with a key in hand. She threw them on the counter and walked away. I was tired of playing games with her so I grabbed them up and gathered my bags together.

As I was walking away, she said "Mrs. Hayward, Oh, excuse me, I forgot *Ms. Jones*. Do you need help to your cottage?" I heard her snicker.

I refused to give her any satisfaction, I continued out the door. After about ten minutes of walking, I wish I did swallow my pride and get help. The cottage was in a secluded area towards the lake. It was surrounded by huge palm trees.

Once I finally arrived, I unlocked the door and went in. It was beautiful. It had an island feel with tropical colors that filled the house.

Finally.

I was getting the overdue vacation that I had longed for. I dropped my bags and ran up the steps. I went to what had to be the master bedroom. The room was huge and fully furnished. It had a large sitting area and a private patio that over looked the water. The in suite bathroom was breath taking. It was decorated with several hues of festive blue and orange coloring. A two person jetted-bathtub and a separate glass tiled shower.

I found two other nicely sized bedrooms with a Jack and Jill bathroom. I didn't know where he wanted me to be, so I decided to be on the safe side and not use the master bedroom. I sat on the bed to attempt to unpack, but my body had other plans. Not even five minutes later I was sound asleep.

Later in the afternoon, I woke up to the melody of *Beyonce's Speechless*, which meant someone had left me a message on my cell phone. I grabbed it from off the table and yawned. I was shocked at how late it was, it was 1p.m. and I had six messages.

Damn, I can't believe I slept that long.

I called my answering machine to check them; they were all from Lorenz. A warm feeling came over me. As I listened, he was worried because I hadn't called and also wanted to let me know that he was leaving for a football game that started at 4p.m. I saved the messages, hung up and dialed his number.

His answering machine picked up on the first ring.

Damn, I really wanted to talk to him.

I just left a message letting him know that I was fine and that I missed him too. I hung up and began to daydream about our experience we had the night before.

I went down stairs to the kitchen because I was getting hungry. I looked in the fridge and it was empty.

Ok.

I grabbed a cup from the cabinet and turned on the faucet to get a drink of cold water. I went into the living room area to open the curtains. The sun was bright.

Then I heard a beeping noise from down the hall. I went to investigate and that's when I found out there was a little office here also. Dr. Hayward had a nice flat screen monitor, fax machine, and copier. Anything you would need to conduct business was in that room. The beeping sound was coming from the fax machine. I took the papers from the tray and it was a note from Dr. Hayward.

"*Sasha, please take this day to enjoy yourself. As you should already know the travelers checks are as good as money here. Don't answer the phones, or use the computer. I will contact you by fax or cell only. Don't go grocery shopping. We will dine out. You are not far from downtown Disney. Go to the park, swim, and do whatever you want just have fun. I'll see you soon, Greg." Greg, wow he actually used his first name."* I guess he was loosening up. I hurried back upstairs to get dressed so I could enjoy the rest of my day.

I went to Disney World and had a blast. I was like a big kid. I had never been so I had a ball. It was close to 9p.m., before I heard from Lorenz. I was enjoying my Limo ride back to the resort when the call came in. I answered excitedly.

"Hello!" I was so in awe of my day, that I forgot that I was supposed to be helping my sister with a bad situation. "Listen to you, you're awfully cheerful."

I caught myself, "Oh...." I laughed it off. "Umm, we were just listening to this guy on the radio. He said something really funny."

"Ok. I miss you and can't wait for you to come back."

I smiled, "I miss you too."

I did miss him even though he had not crossed my mind because I was having so much fun. He went on to say how his brother had to go out of town tomorrow and he left him in charge of my caseload.

I felt bad.

He was stuck doing my work while I'm out here living it up with Greg. He asked me if I had any idea when I would be back. I told him I wasn't sure I just knew it would be sometime that week. We talked on the phone for over an hour getting to know each other more. Before he hung up he told me he was taking me on a real date.

A non-sexual date.

I told him I could not wait. We said our goodbyes and hung up.

I decided that I wanted to take a bath in that huge hot tub in the master bedroom. Dr. Hay...I mean Greg wouldn't mind if I used it...he did say have fun and enjoy myself. I ran hot water and added *Love Spell* bubbling bath oil. I loved that fragrance. I turned on the jets and slowly lowered myself in the tub. I opened the blinds to the window overlooking the lake. The water was so soothing. As I lay there, the jets massaged my body allowing me to relax more and clear my mind.

I was so relaxed that I didn't even realize I wasn't alone. I felt hands, nice strong hands massaging my temples. I opened my eyes and looked up into Greg's eyes. He smiled and kissed my forehead. He walked around to the side of the tub. He had on cream linen pants and a cream linen shirt. It looked so good against his mocha skin. I swear that man didn't look a day over 35, he looked amazing. He reminded me so much of Lorenz. I felt my body heat rising as I looked at him.

I think he read my mind.

He began to undress, "Can I join you?"

Without any guilt I gave him consent. He climbed into the tub behind me and whispered in my ear for me to relax. I leaned back on him and let him do his job.

Chapter 7

Awesome! That's the only word that I could use to describe Greg. Absolutely awesome!

After our bath, he led me to the master bedroom and laid me on the bed. Our bodies were dripping wet. I laid there waiting to see what he would do next. I just prayed that he wouldn't pull out a belt or any type of restraint. He knelt at the edge of the bed and pulled my body towards his face. He placed my legs on his shoulders, and began to suck on my inner thighs. My pulse increased as he made his way to taste my wetness. He flicked my clit with his tongue. I quivered as he took his time and explored my pussy with his lips and tongue. He sucked each lip until they swelled. He slurped on my juices as they escaped from my opening.

I moaned deeply.

He gently gnawed the hood of my clit awakening every nerve in my body. An overwhelming sense of stimulation riveted through my body like a shockwave. My legs locked around his neck as my body convulsed in ecstasy.

That was his signal to go in for the kill; he began to suck on my clit like a baby would a pacifier. I let out screams of passion. I could not control myself any longer. I started to grind my pussy wildly hoping he would loosen his grip. He locked in like a pit bull. He shook up my pussy with the lashing of his tongue. I tried to move back but he pulled me in closer.

I was helpless. I was on my 5th climax and he was still going at it like a beast.

I screamed out his name, "GREG! PLEASE! STOP! OH GOD! YOU WIN! YOU WIN!"

Words that didn't make any sense flew from my mouth. I couldn't believe the effect he was having on me. All this from oral pleasure! My legs were numb. He continued to feast on me for hours before I fell into a deep sleep. In the middle of the night, he awakened me and sent me to my room.

I could not move. My legs were limp. I was helpless.

He saw that I was in bad shape and helped me up. No words were exchanged as he helped me to my room. He just kissed my forehead, and walked out. Moments later, I was sleep.

I woke up gasping for air. I sat up on the side of the bed trying to catch my breath. I needed water. I held my chest coughing as I went to the kitchen. I looked on the dining room table, it was set up. I grabbed a bottle of water that was on the center and drank it. I took a deep breath. It had gotten stuffy in the house, I needed a fan on or a window opened. I turned on the ceiling fan and walked over to the dining room table. A platter was made with biscuits, bacon, ham, pancakes, sausage, tropical fruits, and much more. A note was next to the plate.

"*Sasha, I ordered breakfast. I'm going to my conference, and then I'm going to play a little golf. I will see you around 5pm for dinner at Olivia's cafe. Go to my room, I have something there for you to wear for the evening. Enjoy your day, Greg.*"

I sat down and made my plate.

Wow, all this food. I know I'm a big girl, but Damn, I'm not going to eat all of this.

I sat down to eat my meal. This was the first real meal I had in days. After I finished I cleared the table and put the leftovers in the fridge. I went upstairs to his room to find the outfit. The phone rang. I was about to answer it but I thought back to the fax and let it ring. I went to the closet and pulled out the bag. Inside there was a beautiful tangerine colored halter sundress, by *Dereon.*

It was stunning.

There was a shoebox next to it. I sat on the bed and opened the box; a huge smile came upon my face as I pulled out a stunning pair of gold and tangerine strap sandals also by the same designer. He has great taste. I checked the shoe size and he was on the money, size 8. I was so amazed by how he knew my clothes and shoe size that I didn't notice the gold *Christion Dior* clutch bag until it fell from the dress bag.

I was going to be sharp tonight.

Greg is something special. This vacation, the gifts, who would have known this was the same man who treated me as if I was nothing but his work slave for years...It had to be something to it.

I carried the clothes to my room to hang them up. I wonder why he never tried to penetrate me or let me touch him. Maybe he had some type of control fetish. Who knows, and who cares. I know I was reaping the benefits both ways. My material needs being met by Greg. My emotional and sexual needs were being met by Lorenz. I literally had the best of both worlds.

Later that evening, I met Greg at Olivia's which was just a few blocks away. I wore the dress and I have to admit it complemented my bronze complexion wonderfully. I looked striking as I strutted down the boardwalk like I was Ticara from *America's Next Top Model.* I ran into the desk clerk from the other day. I felt her eyes on me.

I smirked and kept it moving.

Once at the restaurant I spotted Greg immediately; he had on a pair of Khaki shorts and a tangerine Polo shirt. We matched. How cute. I walked over to the table. He got up and pulled the chair out for me.

"What did you do today?"

"Not much I just sat around the lake enjoying the sites, and I took a trip to the Spa to be pampered." I smiled.

I left out the fact that I talked to Lorenz for hours out by the lake. He made me laugh all day as we talked about everything from the clients to Greg and his arrogant behavior.

"Why are you smiling like that? Do you have something up your sleeve Ms. Lady?" I snapped back to reality. I forgot that

Greg was even there.

"Oh no. It's just everything that's between us, it's just so amazing that's all." I lied. He didn't look as if he believed me.

"So, how was your day?"

He talked about the conference. He sounded like his regular lifeless self as he talked about his work. I nodded and acted as if I was interested in what he said. We ordered our food; I ordered the crab cakes and he ordered lobster. I have no idea why we opted to sit on the deck, I hate flies. I couldn't enjoy my food with insects flying around. We ate in silence.

"Have you talked to Lorenz?" I froze.

I sat my fork down and wiped my mouth. "Excuse me?"

He asked me again, "Have you talked to Lorenz?" He never looked up from his plate he continued to eat.

"No." I lied.

"I told him to call you from time to time, to update you on your patients' progress," he sounded a little agitated. I didn't want him to be angry with him so I changed my story up.

"Well I don't know if he called or not, I haven't really used my cell." I pushed my plate away. I had lost my appetite.

Greg continued to enjoy his food.

I sat back, downed Apple Martini's, and listened to the Calypso band play. By the time he was done with his meal, I was feeling it and so was he. He held my hand as we walked back to our place. We were silent and enjoyed the warm Fall breeze. I had to take my shoes off because I couldn't walk straight; I was really feeling it.

Before Greg opened the door, he leaned and whispered, "I would like it very much if you would accompany me in my room."

I did not know if that was a direct order or if I had a choice in the matter. It didn't make a difference one way or the other, because the way I was feeling I was definitely ready to relive last night's experience.

I followed him upstairs to his room. I closed the door behind me and loosened my dress from around my neck. I let the dress fall and stepped out of it. Greg opened the patio door and I followed. As I was walking I noticed myself in the mirror. At that point I didn't see the chubby chick, I saw a voluptuous vixen. I felt beautiful. I was suddenly empowered.

When I stepped out the door I was greeted by Greg and his very naked body. His body glistened in the moonlight. He grabbed my ass and lifted me around his waist. He pinned me against the glass door and buried his head in between my breasts. He was biting my nipples and squeezing my ass. I started to think about Lorenz as he was enjoying my body. Then in the midst of thoughts, I let out a passionate moan. Greg had entered me. I was in disbelief. This was the first time he ever actually penetrated me.

Damn, he doesn't have on a condom.

I wanted to tell him to wait, but it was too late. He was hitting that spot right. He continued to bury his face in my tits as he rammed deeper into the abyss. My head began to hit the glass. I held him tighter around the neck and locked my legs around his waist. It seemed as if the tighter I held on, the harder he would buck. I couldn't do anything but hold on for dear life as he wailed away on my insides. I see we were back to the pain is pleasure series. I started to cream everywhere.

Back to back he was fucking the shit out of me. His dick wasn't as big as his brothers, but it was a good 8 to 9 inches long, and he was working it. My head was bobbing around like I was ready to catch whiplash. He started to grunt as he moved faster and grinded deeper. I tried to hold in my cries of bliss. I had to remember we were outside, but I couldn't control it.

Greg began to speak, "Is this my pussy? This is the best dick you ever had, say it!" I tried, but I couldn't say anything the way my head was jerking around. He took one of his fingers and stuck it in my ass. I came again.

Greg was sweating like a hog, and he was like an energizer bunny, he kept going and going and going. Then the ultimate happened. I felt him let loose all inside of me. His body quivered as he shot his cum all in me. We both stood there to catch our breath before he let me down. He squeezed my ass a few more times. He gave me a tender peck on the lips; he slapped me on the ass and walked towards the bathroom. I followed behind mesmerized.

He turned to me and said, “Go get dressed. You have a plane to catch....”

I stood there. He turned on his shower. “Greg, I don't understand.” I felt used.

“What is it that you don't understand? Your things are packed and there's a car waiting for you at the lobby. I will talk to you on Friday when I get back home.”

I was fuming. I couldn't believe he wasn't even going to have the decency to let me freshen up. I put the dress on and grabbed my things. I walked to the lobby in disbelief.

Who the hell packed my shit?

When I got to the lobby, sure enough a car was there waiting. I asked the driver to wait while I went to the bathroom to freshen up. I walked in the lobby and I saw the smart-ass clerk. She smiled at me while talking to a woman who looked very familiar. As I got closer, I realized who she was. It was Mrs. Camille Hayward.

Her back was to me but I knew it was her, by her signature realistic Pocahontas weave that hung down the middle of her back. I could not let her see me here. I hurried into the car and ordered the driver to pull off.

Chapter 8

That black bastard.

He had just screwed the hell out of me and threw me out like a two dollar hoe. I was humiliated and felt cheap. I cannot believe I was actually about to go back and kick the door in and punch him in the face. Thank God, I came to my senses. I thought about that stank clerk smiling sarcastically as she talked with Mrs. Hayward. She was probably the one who packed my shit.

Bitch.

He actually rushed me out, for her. I understand that she was his wife, but come on he hadn't been out the pussy for a good five minutes. This situation was starting to be a little too much for me. I was slowly losing control and making bad decisions. I still can't believe what I did later that night. I tried so hard to remember him, but everything was too fuzzy.

I spoke with Lorenz a few days after I returned home. I let him continue to believe I was in Atlanta. I wasn't ready to face him yet.

Tonight, he was taking me to the American Grill in Chadds Ford, PA for dinner. The whole time I was getting ready for my date, my weekend replayed in my head over and over.

How could something so wonderful come crashing down so fast?

I thought about Camille, I had to admit, she was a beauty. I see why he was married to her. She was just a few years older than me. I was 31, so I think she was either 36 or 37. She was about 5'8", flawless chocolate skin, thin, and kept herself up. She reminded me of the girl Kenya Moore from the Pantene shampoo commercials. She was what some would call high maintenance. She kept a luxurious lace run weave and stayed up with the latest fashion. Maybe that's why he was so stylish. She was no slouch. She had her own money; she was in the million-dollar club with Remax Realtors. I found myself getting a tad bit jealous so I had to check myself. This woman didn't do anything to me. I had just slept with her husband. I had no right to be mad. I zipped my pants and put on my blazer. It was cold up here; It wasn't even mid September and it was about 50 degrees outside. I missed the warm weather already. I sat at the kitchen table sipping tea waiting for my date.

I heard loud music coming from my front entrance. Lorenz had just pulled up in his truck. He was blasting Jay Z's CD. You could hear John Legend singing background.

"*The places that we can....Do you wanna ride with me?*"

He still had some young boy in him. He drove a navy blue fully loaded 2006 Lincoln, Navigator. I had to admit, it was hot. I didn't give him a chance to ring the bell. I darted out the house and he was waiting with open arms. He gave me a long, hot, passionate kiss.

"I missed you so much" he said.

"I missed you too."

He opened the door for me and we headed to our destination. Once we arrived we were seated and ordering our food and drinks.

"So how much did you miss me?" I teased. He showed his dimples.

Aww, he was so cute. He held my hands in his.

"Don't ever leave me like that again. Next time I want to go with you."

I felt guilty. "I'm not going anywhere again without you," I assured him.

"Sasha, I have a question. Why did you want me to have sex with you in front of Greg that night? I mean, I am freaky, and I'm not judging you, but I want to be with you. All that violence with sex and voyeurism; I'm just not with it."

I turned away from him and looked out the window.

That damn Greg. What was he up to? I let it go.

"I don't know; I guess I have been going through something lately. I'm not usually like this." I said flatly.

Greg was playing me. He set this shit up. He knew his brother was into me, so he wanted to make me look like some type of whore. I was livid.

"Tell me about your childhood with Greg growing up." This deceit made my curiosity grow.

Now, Lorenz looked uncomfortable. He let go of my hands and sat back. He was saved because our food came. He stuffed his mouth immediately. I let it go, for now. There's definitely an issue between the two and I was going to find out.

We continued small talk throughout dinner, and he drove me home. We pulled up in front of my house. There was dead silence.

"Will you stay the night with me?" I grabbed his hand, "I want you to stay with me."

He sighed, "Sasha, I told you I didn't want to make this about sex."

"I just want you to hold me. I don't want to be alone. But, it's up to you."

I got out the truck and walked to my door. I went to shut the door, but he grabbed a hold of me gently.

"Wait," he whispered softly and followed me out the truck.

We made passionate love into the wee hours of the morning, and fell asleep in each other's arms. The next morning I got up and made some breakfast for us. I was making his plate, when I felt hands around my waist, and my neck being kissed. I turned around to return the kiss and I dropped the spatula.

Those were not Lorenz's hands they were Greg's.

I whispered, "How did you get in here?"

I snatched away from him.

Without saying a word he grabbed me by the arm and dragged me into my powder room.

"Greg, what the fuck is wrong with you?"

All respect I had for him was out the door. He was in complete violation and he invaded my home.

He smiled. "I missed you baby. I see you couldn't wait for me. I told you I would be back today."

It was Friday...Damn.

"You better get out my damn house!"

He gave me a look as if to say *yeah right,* and slipped his hand under my robe.

"Mmm, Daddy missed you," he moaned as he violated me.

"What about your wife? How could you miss me when you had her for company?" He ignored my comment.

"Turn around and give me my pussy", he demanded.

"What are you crazy? I have company."

"I know and I will let you get back to Lorenz as soon as you give me what belongs to me. You don't want him to see us like this, so you need to give me what's mine. I don't mind sharing." He said callously.

My eyes were stinging with tears. He was right I didn't want Lorenz to witness this, especially not after what we shared last night. I turned around and bent over the sink. He grabbed my breasts and dropped his pants and rammed his manhood in me. I cried silently within as he had his way. He squeezed my ass and began to pump faster. I had come twice already.

Damn.

I didn't enjoy what was happening mentally, however my body had its own terms. When he was finished, he dressed and handed me an envelope.

"I will see you tomorrow, in your office by 8 a.m."

I nodded.

"One last thing you need to learn to lock your doors, there's crazy people out here."

What have I gotten myself into?

I knew I had to pull myself together before Lorenz came down. I grabbed hand towel and soap and washed his fluids away. I went to the kitchen and continued to finish what I started. Once I was finished, I went into my living room and sat quietly on the chair holding the letter in my hand. I opened the envelope; it was a new work schedule. I now had Wednesday's and Sunday's off. There was a note inside.

"Sasha, I really enjoyed our time together this weekend. Sorry you had to leave in a rush, but Camille found out I had a conference in Orlando so she wanted to surprise me. I had someone tip me that she was coming, but I had to spend one more night with you before she came. Please forgive me. Don't worry, that will never happen again because Tuesday night is now our time. You will leave straight from work and meet me at the Embassy Suites, by the airport. We will have no interruptions. Greg."

I crumbled the letter and cried.

Chapter 9

The holiday season is usually not my best time of the year. I would suffer depression from loneliness; I had no family. I had a friend from high school, we used to talk all the time and spend holidays together. That is until she got married, and moved clear across the country. Now I just receive Christmas and birthday cards. So after that, I became involved deep into my work. I had no one to share time with, until now. Lorenz and I have been official for about a month now. He was so sweet, a perfect gentleman. I felt bad about what I was doing to him.

My dates with Greg were also official. Every Tuesday, I would go to the airport, have dinner and fuck. It was nothing like what Lorenz and I shared. He never showed me any type of affection. We would shower together, and then he would pleasure me orally, and fuck the shit out of me; with no condom might I add. One night he had the nerve to tell me I better use some type of protection with Lorenz because he didn't feel comfortable with me sleeping with him raw.

I completely blew his statement off. He had a lot of nerve; he needs to worry about that scandalous wife of his.

Yes, *Scandalous*.

Lorenz had told me all about her. How she sleeps around, and attends swinger parties. He said Greg knows everything, but he doesn't want to let her go. He even told me how she tried to come on to him. He said he told his brother, and Greg actually gave him the go ahead to do it. I couldn't believe it.

Of course he said he didn't. I don't know if I believed that or not because she was beautiful. But what would I care that was before my time.

Thanksgiving was in two days and I was going to cook for Lorenz. I was excited! My first Thanksgiving with a man… *my* man!

I had taken off work early because I had a doctor's appointment with my GYN. I had to admit, when I found out about Camille's lifestyle, I had to get checked out. I didn't need any surprises.

I lay on the table wearing nothing but a hideous paper gown. They never managed to go around my ass. Dr. Cho was swabbing away taking cultures. Like every woman, I hated this.

"So, how is the practice coming along?" He wanted to converse while probing me.

"It's good Dr. Cho."

"So... have your cycles become regular yet?"

"No they haven't."

See, I have a little issue with my periods. I only come on once or twice a year. They said it was hormones. I have been like this since I was 22.

"So, what are you going to do about that Ms. Jones?"

"I have no idea Dr. Cho."

His head came from between my legs. He went over to his metal tray and put gel all over his gloved fingers. He placed two fingers in me and pressed on my stomach. That's the only time I dislike a man touching me. He was doing it a little longer for some reason.

"Ms. Jones. Did you know your cervix is closed?"

I thought to myself, *how the hell would I know that*?

"No...No, I didn't Dr. Cho. What does that mean?"

He went over to his nurse to set up lab work. "Ms. Jones, go to the bathroom and give me a urine sample."

Immediately I thought the worst.

I got something. What if it's AIDS, or Herpes, Oh my God?

I went to pee in the cup and brought it back to Dr. Cho. He took the specimen with him and told me to get dressed and meet him in his office.

I was nauseated. I was burning. My money was on that nasty ass Camille. My head was buried in my hands when Dr. Cho came in his office with a stack of papers in his hands. I was embarrassed; I've went to this man for years, and now I have to face him.

"Ms. Jones you'll be 32 this year correct?" I nodded my head.

"This means with you being a little overweight, and your age being a factor. It will put you at high risk."

High Risk! *Oh God, it's bad.*

"Congratulations, Sasha you're going to be a mom."

I drove home crying the whole time. I can't have a baby now. This is all wrong.

Oh My God, Who is the dad?

I was having sex on the regular basis with both of them. Greg was a once a week, but he was up in me letting loose several times in one night. Lorenz, he practically moved in except for Tuesday's. Greg made him do an overnight shift at the Wilmington Hospital in Delaware. He had his connects. I felt like one of my patients. I felt like I was about to have a breakdown. Abortion was out of the question; I wanted a family.

But God why now? Why is this happening?

I didn't even go back to work. I went upstairs drew all the curtains and laid in complete darkness.

Bang, Bang, Bang!

Someone was knocking on my door. I ignored it. There it was again, this time even louder. I didn't want to budge. I checked my alarm clock; it was 10:25p.m. I continued to lay there. Then I heard a siren, and someone talking over a loud speaker.

"Ms. Jones, if you are in there, please come to the door, or we are coming in!!"

It's the police! Why would they be here?

I jumped out of bed and ran to my door. When I opened it I saw Greg, Lorenz, and two police officers on my lawn. Lorenz ran to hug me, but the officer stopped him.

"Uhh...Ms. Jones, are you alright? Is anyone in there with you?" He had a suspicious look on his face.

"No, I mean, yes I'm fine, and no, no ones in my house."

"Uh...We were called because your friends here said you haven't showed up for work, and they came here several times and called and couldn't reach you. Uh...are you *sure* you're ok? Do you need to talk to someone?" He raised his eyebrow as if I was trying to hide something.

"No, I'm fine. I've just been tired...I didn't realize it's been that long and my ringer has been off."

"Well, next time ma'am let someone know you're ok. These fellas were pretty worried about you."

He then turned away and motioned for his partner to leave. I walked back in the house with Greg and Lorenz hot on my heels. I went to the kitchen to make a cup of tea. Greg went first.

"Ms. Jones, we were worried about you. You had an appointment Tuesday evening, which you didn't show up for. Your client was concerned."

Client, yeah right.

He was the damn client.

"Is everything Ok? You know you can talk to me, I'm not only your boss, I'm your friend." I poured my tea rolling my eyes.

Lorenz took the cup from my hands and hugged me tightly. "I was so worried about you. Why didn't you answer your phone? Don't ever scare me like that again. I know the holidays are hard for you, but please don't shut me out."

I turned to Greg, "Thank you for your concern, Dr. Hayward. I will be back to work after the holiday. I hope you and your family enjoy your Thanksgiving."
I wanted him to leave and hoped he got the idea.

Instead, he said, "About Thanksgiving, did Lorenz tell you that you'll be dining with us? Oh, I guess he didn't get a chance to, sorry about that bro. So, I will see the both of you tomorrow around 5p.m. Enjoy your evening."

When he was gone I gave Lorenz a piece of my mind.

"I am not going to his house! I thought you wanted me to cook for you! I thought we were having dinner here!" I snapped.

He looked a little bothered by my attitude.

"First off, I don't hear from you for a day and a half, you don't answer the phone, door, or anything. Greg calls and tells me that you skipped out on a client. What if they were suicidal? You were not there for them! Instead you were up here having your own damn pity party! That's selfish! Tomorrow is Thanksgiving. I hear nothing from you, and I didn't know if our plans were still on or not. I tried to do you a favor, so you could relax."

"Yeah…well how would you feel if you just found out you were pregnant…"

Damn, did I just say that?

I didn't mean for it to come out, not yet. Not like this. He was stunned.

"Pregnant! Baby we're having a baby?" He hugged me.
"Baby I'm so sorry. How far are you? Oh My God! I am so happy! I can't wait to tell Greg."

"No!" I pleaded. "I don't want anyone to know yet."

He agreed that we would keep it to ourselves, until I was in the clear. I thought to myself, I would never be in the clear about this. We went to bed that night and he was gentle with me, taking his time. He didn't want to hurt the baby.

When we both reached our climax, he whispered, "I knew you were the one, I'm going to make you my wife. Our child won't be a bastard." I pretended to fall asleep and he held me until morning.

Chapter 10

Of course, I agreed to attend Thanksgiving dinner at the Hayward's. God knows I did not want to be there. This would be the first time I went to his house. I heard that it was a sight to see. I remember how Karyn would gloat about how she had been invited frequently to his mini mansion. She would go on and on about the five acres of land he had with a private entrance. The way she went on about it you would have thought it was her home.

We pulled into the neighborhood and I wasn't impressed. The homes were huge and beautifully landscaped, but they were just a step up from what I had. We rode through until we came to a fork in the road. He took a sharp left and we traveled down a secluded, spiral-graveled road, which had tall trees that hovered over the road in an arch form making it look as if we were in a tunnel made of leaves. An eerie feeling came over me. I felt like I was in a horror movie and Jason or Freddy was about to jump out the woods. I inched over closer to Lorenz and squeezed his free hand. He squeezed mine gently.

"Creepy right?" he laughed.

I nodded my head and laughed nervously.

We were now approaching the end of the road and I noticed the sky lighting back up. He slowed down as we approached a mailbox that had the words Conners-Hayward. The road curved to the right and my eyes almost popped from my head. A light beamed down from the sky beaming down on the most gorgeous house I had ever seen. It reminded me of a modern plantation house with the large beams on the front porch. Exotic flowers, trees and flowers surrounded the home. Now I see *exactly* what Karyn was talking about.

Lorenz parked, and opened the door for me. I felt like a movie star walking up the steps to this fabulous home. I couldn't help but wonder how in God's name they could afford this. I know it had to be close to a million dollars. I know Dr. Hayward was well paid but goodness I didn't think it was like that.

Lorenz went to open the door but before he had the chance to put the key in, it opened and we were greeted by Camille's daughter, Starla. She didn't look anything like her mother. For one she was pale, with ice blue eyes, she was very petite. She reminded me a little of the girl New-New from ATL. She had naturally curly hair that was pulled back tightly in a pony tail that hung to her mid back. To look at her you would automatically think *snob.* That is until she spoke.

"Hey Unc, they back in the dining room. Oh yeah, let me warn you my mom is drunk as hell. So she is actin' a damn fool." She said smacking her gum.

Did this little girl just curse? *Wow that didn't sound quite charming, and was that a tongue ring in her mouth*?

I heard they were paying all this money for her schooling, but she sounded straight hood when she spoke. She followed us into the dining room.

I admired the house as we walked through. It seemed more like a museum than a home. It was very spacious, and empty. It seemed like they had only a few things in each room. The colors a basic white, red, and black theme played throughout the Great Room. All of the furniture was contemporary looking as if it came straight from a high fashion magazine. I wasn't surprised it was said that Mrs. Hayward was high maintenance.

When we reached the dining room, Camille looked as if she were tore up from the floor up. Even in her drunken nature, she was still stunning. Today she had her weave pulled up in a elaborate up-do with a few loose curls hanging in her face. She wore a black wrap dress, which cut low in the front exposing her cleavage that was barely there. Greg was sitting with his laptop on the dinner table, wearing a Cliff Huxtable charcoal sweater and a pair of gray slacks.

"Hey Renzo," she slurred. She looked me up and down. "Is this the new one? I didn't know you were a chubby chaser." She chuckled and went back to drinking her drink.

I wanted to say so is your husband.

Lorenz pulled out my chair and leaned over, "She's just jealous, ignore her."

I wanted to switch my side because she was sitting directly across from me. "You look familiar. Do I know you?"
The glass of wine dangled loosely in her hands as she lifted it to her lips. I hesitated before I spoke. My mind went back to the resort.

Greg spoke up.

"She works for me Camille, that's Sasha Jones."

"Oh, I know you...I remember now. You were a little smaller and your hair was shorter. You have nice hair. What you a mulatto or something?"

I tried to keep my composure. She had the nerve. From the looks of it, her darling daughter looked as if she had a little cream in her.

"No, my dad was from Panama and my mother was African American."

She snickered.

"That's still mulatto, honey." She looked towards the kitchen and changed the subject. "Are they done in there? They need to come on with this food. I have no time for this. I have a party in Baltimore to attend." she said like she was about to snap.

"Let me go check."

Lorenz hurried to the kitchen to see what was going on.

"Mrs. Hayward, you didn't cook?"

She looked as if I spit on her.

"Cook, me cook! Oh no honey, caterers...that's how we do it around here. I am a busy woman. Miss Sasha, I have no time to cook, clean, and whatever else you chicks do."

She was so ghetto fabulous. She really put on a front in public. She had no class at all. Lorenz came back in. He told us they were bringing the food out now. Good, I thought, I just want to get this over with so we can leave. Greg removed the laptop from the table.

"So Sasha, what do you have planned for the New Year?"

"I don't know yet Dr. Hay--" He cut me off.

"We are not at work, you can address me as Greg. I mean you're practically family. The way you and Lorenz have been all over each other."

He was being sarcastic. Camille chimed in.

"Wow, so you two *are* exclusive. Ok Renzo...I see how you are. What you don't like chocolate no more?" She turned her attention to me and smiled slyly.

"You want to trade sometimes?"

She was serious. I could see it in her eyes. I didn't respond. The food came out and everyone made their plates. I sat picking at my plate, while everyone chit chatted and threw out slick comments. I couldn't eat.

Greg put his fork down. "Sasha, is everything alright? You barely touched your food."

"I am fine Greg just a little tired."

Lorenz spoke up, "I am about to head out Sasha needs her rest."

I gave him a sharp look. He shouldn't have said that.

"Rest? For what?" he asked. "Are you sick?"

"No, I'm fine. We can stay, I'm fine." I wanted to drop that issue, immediately. So, I said to Camille. "What type of party are you going to?"

Greg glared at her.

She rolled her eyes and said, "Only the best kind of party; Where your fantasy can become reality." A seductive smile came across her face, "You want to come?"

"No, she doesn't want to come Camille!" Greg snapped. Camille began to laugh.

"Wow, Greggy. What's up your ass? It might be good for her, for you too Renzo." She was gazing at him seductively.

"Damn, I'm sorry. I always get lost looking at you. You and Greggy look so much alike. Be careful, one day I just might mistake you for him, and well you know, Starla's at the table." There was that God awfully shrieking laugh again, "Don't you think they look alike Miss Sasha?"

I nodded.

She leaned over towards me and smiled, "When he's fucking you, do you sometimes imagine that he's Greg?"

My eyes felt like they were about to pop from my head. I couldn't believe she said that.

"Camille! That's enough!" Lorenz became angry.

"Sorry, Renzo. I mean damn, you two look just alike." She had a point they did look alike.

"Well Mrs. Hayward they are brothers."

She busted out laughing again. "Yeah, I know."

She looked at Greg, "Brothers, Brothers, Brothers. That's why we can just keep it in the family. Are you with it Miss Sasha? I know you're a freak; it's always the shy quiet types. We have BBW's at our parties."

Starla got up from the table. I think she had enough. I know I did. I stood up, and Lorenz followed behind me.

"No, don't leave. I'm sorry...I'm sorry...You know we have a pole in the basement. I can give you some live entertainment. I mean if you guys need to livin' things up, I'm always game. Right Greggy? Tell Renzo you'll let me out to play."

"Camille, that's enough. Greg, thanks man, but we got to go." Lorenz said with a serious look on his face.

Camille immediately grabbed her glass and took a deep gulp and waved goodbye. Greg was fuming. His eyes were fixed on Camille; she was in for it, but from the looks of things, I think she would enjoy it....

Chapter 11

"Are you going to your sisters for Christmas?" Lorenz asked while sitting on the lazy boy in my office. I was finishing up a few case notes before I left for the day.

"My sisters? What sister?"

He had totally caught me off guard. He sat up in the chair.

"I guess the one in Georgia...that's the only sister I know about." I had forgotten about that lie. I tried to play it off.

"Oh...No. She and her husband will be in Aspen." I said nonchalantly. I couldn't believe how that lie just rolled off my tongue with ease.

"Well, did you tell her about the baby?"

I looked away from the computer. "I thought we were not going to talk about the baby right now," I snapped.

"Well excuse me! You know Sasha...I thought you would be more excited about our baby!"

His feelings were hurt. I ignored him and continued typing. I haven't been in the best mood lately. The pregnancy, Greg, and the show Camille put on last week were too much. So I took a little time off for myself. Lorenz came over to my desk and stood next to me.

"Sasha, baby, why are you being this way? You haven't let me touch you since that night you told me about the baby...Are you still mad about Thanksgiving? I apologized over and over for making you go and--."

I cut him off...my tone was sharp, “You didn't make me do anything! I went because I wanted to...As for Camille's performance...I could care less....” I rolled my eyes just thinking about her behavior.

He laughed.

“What's so fucking funny?”

I was pissed. I couldn't believe he was sitting here laughing at me, and I didn't know why.

“You know what? If I'm so fucking funny...you can get out!” I waved my hand for him to shoo.

The smile faded from his face, “Hold on...Who you think you're talking to Sasha? You need to calm your ass down! Don't curse at me! I don't curse at you!” He was irritated.

I snickered, “So what you're mad...I laughed. So what Renzo!” I said imitating Camille.

He didn't laugh. I moved from my desk and sat on his lap. “Aww, baby I'm sorry,” I apologized. He didn't respond. I started kissing his bald head. He had recently cut it all off. “I'm sorry Mr. Clean.”

He tried not to laugh. I slid off his lap and locked my office door. No one was on this floor and Greg was at the hotel, so we would have no interruptions. I walked over to him seductively. I unbuttoned my blouse.

“I got something that will make you feel good,” I teased.

He tried to act like he wasn't with it, but I knew him like a book. He was all for it. I knelt on the floor in front of him, unzipped his pants, and pulled out my best friend. I kissed around the head slowly. I flicked my tongue up and down his shaft before taking him deeply. He ran his fingers through my hair. I took him in again and further this time. It was getting good to him; I felt him growing more in my mouth. He stood up and pushed my head further trying to get me to take it all. That wasn't the best idea because before I knew it I vomited all over his dick. He jumped back.

“Sash! Oh baby, you Ok?”

I was embarrassed. I jumped up and ran to the bathroom. I washed my face. I heard a knock at the door.

"Sasha, it's cool. Come out baby...It's ok...I understand." I let him in and he held me as I cried. "I am so embarrassed, I'm sorry for everything."

"It's ok; at least we weren't kissing when it happened." We both laughed. "I'll have a janitor clean the office. I got to head out to work; will you be alright getting home?" He asked sincerely.

I nodded.

Before we walked away he said, "Sasha...I love you."

That was the first time he ever said that to me.

I mouthed, "I love you too." I looked in the mirror. I had to end this charade. I was determined to end things with Greg tonight. When I arrived, Greg was in his usual spot, on the sofa typing on the lap top.

"Hey stranger…."

I ignored him.

I took off my coat and sat in the recliner. "Greg, we need to talk--."

He interrupted. "I apologize for my wife. She gets a little out of hand when she drinks. She can't help herself."

I sighed and took a deep breath.

"Greg I'm not talking about Camille, I'm talking about our situation. I'm not doing it anymore."

He continued typing. Without looking at me he nonchalantly said, "What Sasha...I didn't hear you...You're not what?"

He knows he heard every word I said. I played along with him by raising my voice up an octave. I was very direct this time.

"I'm not fucking you anymore."

A silly smile spread across his face. He backed away from the laptop, folded his hands behind his head and chuckled.

"Sasha, you're right, you're not fucking me. I am fucking you and I will continue to fuck you as much as I want. I mean you *are* carrying *my* baby." He was so sure of himself.

I instantly felt ill. My stomach began to knot up, and saliva filled my mouth. I wanted to vomit.

"Who told you that? How did you know?" I was frantic.

"Sasha, I'm a doctor. Plus I saw the paper work on your dining room table. So when is the first ultra sound? I need to be there." He said placidly.

I jumped in his face, "You're not coming near my baby!" I shouted. He stood up. We were now face to face.

"Sasha you need to calm down and I hope you know that when you're further along you're going to stop sleeping with my brother. I just don't feel comfortable with him inside you while my baby is there...So just sit and relax, this will work out." He sat back down and picked up his lap top.

I continued to stand over him. "I'm not letting you control me, Greg...your brother, wants to marry me." Greg laughed out loud.

I didn't see anything humorous about what I just said. I was really livid now.

"He's not marrying you...once he finds out your pregnant, he's going to drop you like a hot pan."

I was perplexed. Then it came to me. He thinks we use protection. He actually thought I listened to him. I played along. I laughed within. The joke would definitely be on him.

"You know what Greg? You're right. He's not going to marry me. I guess you win, Greg. "So, what will Camille say, when she finds out about the baby?" I said mischievously.

"You know what? You don't worry about that." He was so cool about things, and it made me want to bust him in the head with something to make him snap. He stood up and walked over to me. He grabbed my arm gently and pulled me from the chair, leading me to the bedroom. My heart began to beat fast; I didn't want this to happen. I had fallen in love with Lorenz. I had to keep reminding myself. *This is the last time.* He laid me on the bed, and started to undo my clothes.

"Sasha, why do you treat me so bad? I thought we had a good thing going."

He spread my legs and slid right into me. He wasn't his usual aggressive self. I guessed he called himself making love. I closed my eyes tightly and thought about Lorenz. I hated myself for actually enjoying the way he made my body feel. I tried not to enjoy it, but there was no way I could hide how I was feeling. What really bothered me was that he knew it.

Chapter 12

The next morning, he woke me up extremely early. "We need to talk."

He was already dressed in his usual gray colored slacks and white crisp oxford with a snug tie. I sat up in the bed. "You have a Masters in Psychology, correct?"

I nodded.

"Did you ever think about going for your Doctorate?"

I have to admit, I had thought about it, but just never had taken any time to do it.

"Well as you know I graduated from Duke University...and I am on their board...and I know the baby is due in June, correct?" He said with an eyebrow raised.

I shook my head in amazement. *Man, he really had things figured out.*

"Well you will be a student there in the fall."

My mouth dropped. Here he goes again trying to control me.

"Earth to Greg...how about Duke is in Durham, NC and I live in West Chester, PA. That's a hell of a commute." I smacked myself in the head jokingly, "Oh, duh. I forgot the main issue. I will have a baby! How am I supposed to do all this?" I shook my head in disbelief.

Being cocky as always, he shrugged his shoulders as if it was nothing, "Easy...your house is being built as we speak, and as for your job, you accepted the position as The Department

Head of Psychology, at Duke University Hospital. You'll be making around six figures with less work to do. I'll let you interview the nannies in April." He was candid with his words. He handed me house plans, and a deed. To my surprise his name was nowhere on it. I was speechless.

"No need to thank me. I want the best for *my* baby. Oh, and Sasha we don't have to meet here anymore. I'll let you have your fun with Lorenz; I know you guys don't have much time left." He winked and disappeared through the door.

I read the papers, everything was legit. He even has a trust fund for the baby. The words he said sunk through my head. *We don't have much time*. Lorenz meant more to me than any of this material stuff. I wasn't going to lose him. No way.

***

"Southwestern Flight 256, Orlando Florida is now boarding."

"That's us." he said. It was Christmas morning and we were in the airport on our way to who knows where. Well I knew where we were headed *now*, and I don't think I am going to like what I was in for...

For the last couple of months, my life had been in disarray. I stepped in a dangerous game full of lust and treachery. Who would have thought I would fall in love, become pregnant, and married all in 3 months. Yes, married. After my last "date" with Greg, he made it plain to me he wouldn't stop until he had me to himself. So I took matters into my own hands. The next day when Lorenz came over to my house, I asked if he was serious about wanting me to be his wife.

He explained how he knew I was the one, and his whole life story of how he basically stalked me from afar for the last year. He apologized again for what happened the night we met officially. I explained to him again, there was no need to apologize I enjoyed it. He also expressed his concern on how it was very important that his child not be a bastard. He wanted to marry me before the child was born, but he wasn't quite sure how I felt. I told him my feelings were the same.

Two days later at The America Grill, he proposed on bended knee and presented me with a little blue box labeled Tiffany & Co. Inside contained a round brilliant with a melee diamond border engagement ring. Everyone who was watching was in awe. An older Caucasian woman came over and said,

"You are one lucky girl! Do you know how much that thing cost?" Everyone burst out in laughter. She was right; the ring was valued at $16,000. I didn't even know he made that type of money. But money wouldn't matter; we were going to be alright thanks to my future brother in law. On Christmas Eve day, we drove to Elkton, Maryland to the Justice of the Peace. So I am now officially Mrs. Sasha Jones-Hayward.

Since we didn't have a big wedding he wanted to take me somewhere. He said it would be a surprise so I agreed. I had taken my vacation time anyway.

When we arrived everything was all too familiar. I was back at Old Key West. He explained that Greg had a time share, and that he asked could he use it for the holiday.

"Greg knows we are here? Did you tell him we were married?"

He had a confused look on his face. "No, not yet. I will tell him when we get home, and I am telling him about the baby also."

I had to remain calm, I was still early on in my pregnancy, so I tried not to stress about anything. When the cab stopped I hopped out of the car and grabbed my bags. I was headed towards the cottage. He was paying the driver and gathering the rest of our things.

He yelled, "Sasha...Sasha, wait you don't know where you're going!"

Damn...I forgot, I had to act like this was all new to me. I waited for him to catch up. I walked behind him.

He chuckled, "Well, at least you were going in the right direction."

I gave him a fake laugh. It was more people here this time; I guess everyone wanted to head to Disney for Christmas. We went inside and he hugged me.

"Do you like it baby?"

He was so excited; he really thought he was exposing me to something fresh. I played into him.

"Yes, baby it's beautiful, everything is wonderful." I walked throughout the house as if it were all new. When I reached the Master bedroom, I ceased at the door. I began to reminisce about Greg and that amazing night we shared out on the patio, I was musing.

"Sasha, are you Ok?" Lorenz came up behind me.

"Oh, I'm fine; I was just looking at this room, it's beautiful." I was still reflecting on my experience I had out there. I had to snap out of it.

"Umm... isn't there some parade going on? I thought you said you wanted to go." His eyes lit up like a pedophile in a kinder-garden class.

"The Walt Disney Christmas Parade. We'll unpack later. Let me call to see when the next shuttle is coming so we can get going."

He went to call the front lobby. I took one more look back into the room. A chill went down my back as I closed the doors on my past.

Chapter 13

The next few days were filled with excitement, and tender moments. Everything was just awesome. The memories that Greg and I shared were fading. Lorenz and I were making new ones. We discussed our plans for the baby. One evening we were talking about names when his mood suddenly changed.

I said, "If it's a girl, we should name her Azariah Ra'Chae." My mother's name was Rachael. He had a funny look on his face but he agreed.

"What happened to your mother?"

"I guess I never really told you about my family. My mother died of cancer when I was thirteen. My Auntie Selma took me in and put me through school, she died right after my high school graduation. I don't have any real siblings. The sister I told you I was visiting was my best friend. She is like family."

I studied his face to see if he was mad that I lied. He didn't seem mad, but he was very quiet. I continued on, "I never knew my father. My mom said he was from Panama and got deported. She never even told me his name. I do have a few cousins that I hear from once in a blue moon...It's basically just me."

He didn't say anything; he just played with a piece of string that was hanging from the table cloth. Something was on his mind, I could tell by the solemn expression he wore. I just couldn't put my finger on what was bothering him. I ran my fingers across his smooth chest.

"I was thinking if it were a boy, we could name him Lorenz

Jr."

He jumped up, and removed my hand from his chest. "No!"

I jumped. I was a little taken back by his reaction. Most men wanted their first son named after them, unless this wasn't his first child.

"You just have to be very careful when naming your children. My grandma always told me that names carry spirits, you know like curses."

He had me completely mystified. What was up with all this C*urses and Spirits?*

"Your grandmother told you that? What was she one of those 'Holiness' people? They're the only people I know who talk that spirit and curse stuff besides people who deal in voodoo."

Maybe I should have inquired more about his past before I rushed to get married.

"Tell me about your family? How was it growing up with the infamous Gregory Hayward?" He seemed to be a little reluctant at first. After a brief moment he took a deep breath.

"I played football in high school. I ended up earning a full athletic scholarship. My home life was normal; my relationship with Greg was, I guess, typical for brothers. He stayed out of my way and I stayed out of his."

"Is that it?"

"Yeah, that's it."

I didn't believe that. It had to be more to it. So I started to ask questions.

"What were your parents like? Where they doctors? I never knew Greg had a brother, are there anymore siblings? Aunts, Uncles...?

He seemed agitated and avoided answering my questions. He rose from the couch. "I'm tired. Tomorrow's New Years Eve and this place turns into party central so we better get some rest."

"Wait Lorenz, I'm not done talking to you?" He continued up the steps and never answered.

I stood there feeling rejected. I can't believe he just left me hanging like that. Something happened between them. I was now even more determined to find out what it was.

***

I woke up to a bunch of bickering back and forth. I rolled over to look for Lorenz, but he wasn't in the bed. I grabbed my robe, went to the hallway, and looked over the balcony. I should have known. It was too good to be true. The devil had to show its ugly face. The first person I saw was Camille, with her fingers all in my husband's face rolling her neck. She wasn't alone she had some woman, and of course "Greggy".

"I know damn well you don't have an attitude Renzo...we have just as much right to be here, matter of fact...THIS IS OUR SHIT! WE WERE BEING NICE TO YOUR ASS LETTING YOU COME DOWN HERE!" she yelled. Greg was in the kitchen talking to their company. He spotted me as I made my way down the steps.

"Good Morning, Sunshine!" He chimed as if there wasn't really going to be a brawl right before his eyes. "Look Camille, look who's finally up." She ignored him and continued to curse out my husband. I wasn't standing for this so I walked in between them.

"Is there a problem Camille because we can leave." I said with an attitude. She calmed herself for a moment.

"No need to leave Miss Sasha...I was telling your ungrateful little boyfriend a thing or two." She snarled "Renzo, I'll deal with you later."

Like hell she would.

She grabbed me by the side of my robe. Jabbing me with her brightly colored daggers she called nails.

"Come here Miss. Sasha. Let me introduce you..." her words stopped when she saw my ring. "JESUS CHRIST! IS THAT A TIFFANY MELEE...SHELLY COME LOOK AT THIS SHIT!"

They were both admiring my ring.

The Shelly chic said, "Is this an engagement ring?" She had a heavy New York accent. Lorenz was ready to speak, but I cut him off.

"Yes, we plan to get married in the summer."

I didn't want him to come out and say anything. That would ruin everything. He didn't understand, I just shook my head. Greg walked over to see what all the fuss was about.

He was wearing a nice blue Polo shirt with a pair of Dockers.

"Oh, that's cute, Lorenz."

"So when were you going to tell me about the wedding? I am the only family you really have left, I should have been the first to know" He had a suspicious look on his face.

Again, I took charge.

"Well, when we came back after the holiday we were going to have an engagement dinner." I lied.

Lorenz stood there trying to figure me out. Greg knew something was up. I could see it. "

"Sasha, how do you like the house? Beautiful isn't it? Have you ever been around this area before?" He was trying to be funny. I rolled my eyes and introduced myself to Shelly.

Shelly was breath taking. She stood about 5'7", bronze complexion, and this ridiculously long auburn weave. She could have passed for a Brazilian version of Beyonce. Her body was well put together; big tits, little waist, wide hips, and a donkey bootie. She looked like she was one of Uncle Luke's dancers. I watched Lorenz sneak a few peeks. She walked over to him and gave him a hug.

"Now I see why you didn't call a sista back. Congratulations."

I cut my eyes at Greg, he was grinning to himself. Camille had a huge smile plastered across her face. I guess I was the only one in the dark.

I cleared my throat, "Am I missing something?"

Camille spoke up. "Oh, it's nothing Miss Sasha, at least nothing you would understand...See Shelly comes to play with us sometimes, and you know...well."

Lorenz cut in. "Shelly and I used to date...it was nothing serious, we just had a few dates."

"Yeah nothing serious, but I wouldn't call what we did dates." She giggled.

She walked over to Camille and whispered something in her ear. They both giggled and made their way upstairs whispering.

I was heated. I could feel the blood heat up in my veins. *What the hell did I get myself into*?

I felt like my brain was on rewind. It just kept playing the conversation back in my head.

I wouldn't call them dates? *They all played together. What was that supposed to mean*?

I held my hand up to my head; it felt like the room was spinning.

"Sasha, are you Ok? Greg moved in close and tried to place his hands on my stomach. I hurried and backed away.

"I'm fine; I just need to lie down." I turned away and ran up the stairs back to our room, fuming. I needed answers now! I sat in the wicker rocker trying to get myself together. Moments later Lorenz appeared with a dumb look on his face.

"You know what...I think we may have rushed into this marriage thing a little too quickly."

I turned and directed my attention to the window focusing on the lake. If I looked at him I knew it wouldn't be long before I broke down emotionally. I spoke calmly and low, I didn't want the freak twins to hear my business. It didn't last long because the thought of them laughing at me kept popping up.

"I mean seriously, I don't know much about you at all...now the ghetto poca-ho-ho, and her side kick think everything is a damn joke...well that I'm a joke."

Tears flowed from my eyes. I couldn't help it, I was hurt.

"I don't understand...I just don't know what I am doing anymore...I'm trying to make things right, I just want to be happy, I want a normal family not this craziness."

I looked at him and noticed tears in his eyes. He walked over to me with his arms stretched He held me as I cried in his arms.

"Baby, we are a family. I promise everything will be fine, you will be happy. When we get home, I will tell you *everything*. I love you Sasha. No more secrets."

I whispered, "No more secrets?"

"Miss Saaa-shaaaa, wake up Miss Saashaa." I opened my eyes and Camille and Shelly were in my face giggling. I wiped my mouth and sat up.

"Miss Sasha...I want you to come with us...Here, I got a bathing suit for you, I know you can fit it. I checked out the closet and found your size."

I wasn't fully awake, and I didn't want to go swimming especially with them. I looked at the suit it was a basic black one piece.

"Umm Camille, I don't want to swim."

Shelly laughed, "Neither do I. I hope you didn't think I was getting my six hundred dollar infusions wet." They both laughed.

Camille threw me the suit. "Here put it on. It's one of them slim suits; you know it holds everything in."

I rolled my eyes in disgust. I didn't want to be bothered. I figured I had to go along with their little charade in order to get them off my back.

"Ok, I'll go."

I waved my hand for them to leave while I got undressed. They didn't budge. "Can you like...leave while I put on my swim suit?"

Camille blurted out, "Why? You don't have nothing we don't...You may have a little more but it's no different." She hi-fived Shelly like her joke was actually funny.

I took my pants and panties off underneath the covers and tried to slide the bathing suit up. It was no use, I would have to stand. I tried to be discreet but they were on me. They both gazed at my body. Shelly came over to assist me.

"Let me help you with that Miss Sasha." I pulled away quickly.

"No, that's ok I can manage"

Shelly stared me up and down. Then she looked at Camille.

"Mee-Mee, she's not *that* fat she could stand a few Pilates but she's not obese." I couldn't believe they were sitting there talking about me as if I wasn't there.

Camille had a disapproving look on her face.

"I guess if you so say so. I have to admit…she does have a nice rack." They giggled.

I was fed up with them already. I didn't know what type of time they were on but I was going to let them know I wasn't down with it ASAP.

"Ok...Are you ready?" I asked. I grabbed a cover up and followed them out.

We ended up in a secluded area on the resort grounds. I didn't remember this from the last time I was here. I didn't even know it existed. It was beautiful; The pool was surrounded by huge marble stones and it had a waterfall. The Jacuzzi was connected to the pool, it was really romantic. We all took our cover-ups off and got into the hot tub. I shouldn't have been surprised by their bathing suites. They were barely there. They both sported Chanel string bikinis. Shelly's ass swallowed up her bikini bottom. It shook like jelly every time she moved. I couldn't understand how her waist could be so small and her ass could be so big. I know it had to be hard for her to buy pants.

Camille's body was fit, everything was in place. She looked like a black Barbie doll. We sat and chit chatted for a while. They even made me laugh a few times. It turned out that Shelly was cool. She was a mortgage broker from New York. I knew it; She was into the same life style that Camille was in. They talked about their parties and work. Even Camille mellowed out some. It was starting to get late and I told them I wanted to head back.

Camille made a suggestion, "Let's play Truth or Dare."

"Truth or dare? Weare grown ass women; we are not in high school." I protested.

"Come on Sash...Let's play." Shelly playfully splashed water in my direction.

I thought about it. What damage could it really do it was just a silly game. "Ok, we can play." This would be a way to find out some more information. "Camille, you go first." I said.

"No the youngest goes first."

That was me. Shelly and Camille were the same age. "Ok, I pick truth."

"Is it true you're fucking my husband?"

"What! No…Camille no! Why would you ask me something like that?" My heart was in my throat.

Did she know?

The serious stare turned into a huge smile. She laughed out loud, "Gotcha!" she was pointing at me laughing. "Girl if you could see the look on your face! You were scared shitless!" They were both cracking up. I was pissed.

"Ok...Ok...Ok my turn," I said.

"No Sasha, it's still my turn." Camille turned to Shelly and asked in a seductive manner. "

Truth or dare?" Shelly answered and of course she said Dare. "I dare you to pleasure yourself." Shelly sat up on the side of the Jacuzzi. She slipped her bikini bottom off revealing her perfectly shaved kitty. Hanging from the hood of her clitoris was a piercing shaped like a dumbbell. She removed her top in a teasing manner, allowing only one firm and perky DD tit to pop out at a time. Her areolas were large and as dark as blackberries which looked odd against her bronze skin. Her nipples were thick and protruding. I came to the conclusion that they were not natural. There was no way that anyone's tits of that size could sit so perfectly. She cupped her right breast and brought it to her mouth and stuck her tongue out which was pierced and began to lick and suck on her own breast.

I couldn't believe what she was doing. I put my head down in shame because for some reason I was becoming fascinated by her actions. I felt movement in the water and that's when I noticed Camille's bathing suit floating on top of the water. Camille had her head buried between Shelly's thighs. From the looks of it I was surprised she could breathe the way her nose and mouth were pressed tightly against her ass and kitty.

I watched the xxx-rated show in amazement. Shelly was really into it. She was pushing Camille's head deeper into her abyss, while she massaged Camille's apple shaped ass with her pedicure feet. I had to catch myself all the slurping and moaning was turning me on. I didn't like feeling that way; not about two chicks anyway. I couldn't keep my eyes off them. I shook my head trying to shake the feeling off.

No, Sasha this is not right. This is not right at all! I hurried out of the Jacuzzi and took off running.

I could have sworn I heard them laughing in the distance.

Chapter 14

When I made it back to the house; I burst through the door, looking for Lorenz. On my way up the steps, I heard voices coming from the office area. I crept towards the door and I heard Greg say…

"You are going to do what I say. Do you understand me? I am the only family you have."

"I'm grown now...I've always done everything you wanted me to do. Just let me be happy for once. You can't keep blaming me for her death."

"Don't let me find out you're keeping secrets from me, because remember I have some secrets too. I know that you don't want them to come out." Greg said in a threatening voice.

I heard footsteps coming to the door. I slid in the closet next to the office. Greg looked around and shut the office doors. When the coast was clear, I left out of the closet. I tried to listen to the conversation but the doors were solid. Nothing could be heard but muffled voices. There was definitely a lot of shit going on within this family.

I wondered.

Whose death were they talking about? Was it their mom, I know Greg took it hard when she died. Secrets, he must have been talking about the baby and my move to N.C.

I know I really had to come clean with him now before Greg did. I just didn't know how.

Later that evening we were supposed to check out the

fireworks for the New Year's celebration. I sat on the bed waiting for Lorenz, but drifted off to sleep. When I woke up, it was 11p.m.

Damn I thought, *why didn't he wake me it's almost time for the countdown.*

I looked around the room, and he was nowhere to be found. That was odd. I decided to check downstairs, maybe he was waiting for me. Then a horrific thought came to my mind.

What if Camille and Shelly told him about what went down at the Jacuzzi earlier? Oh God. He would be pissed. I didn't even tell him I was going to hang out with them.

I had to get to him before they could do any damage. I just pray that I wasn't too late. I ran out of the room and made it only to the top the staircase before I was distracted by noises coming from the master bedroom. For some reason, I felt myself being drawn to room; like I was bewitched.

I peeked around the corner and noticed the door was wide open. Candles and incense were lit all around the room. Large pillars with burning candles, where at each corner of the bed. In the middle of the bed Greg laid while his manhood was being engulfed in Camille's mouth. Shelly sat straddled across his face, winding her body seductively. Shelly arched her back as Greg drove his fingers deeply into her plump bottom, causing a rippling effect to take place.

I couldn't take my eyes off of them. I felt a pulsating sensation between my legs. Chills ran through my body arousing emotions and feelings, the display of pornographic exhilaration had me spellbound.

Camille removed Greg's erect dick from her mouth and stood at the side of the bed. Her dark skin shimmered from beads of sweat that covered her body. Greg continued to satisfy Shelly causing her to buck wildly as he man handled her pussy with his experienced tongue. No words were shared amongst the trio just moans, and cries of eccentric elation; which was like fine music to my ears. I was mesmerized by the melody of their erotic symphony. After a loud scream and quickened convulsive movements, Shelly went limp and plummeted to the side of the bed.

Camille stood there breathing rapidly waiting to be caught up in Greg's rapture. Greg arose from the bed reminding me of a black Adonis. He grabbed Camille by the waist and swept her off her feet without effort. She wrapped her long legs around his waist as they kissed passionately like two teenagers madly in love.

Visions of the night we shared danced through my mind. Jealousy overtook me as I watched Greg caress and show affection to his wife; the kind of affection he never once showed me. The one who did everything he wanted without question, the one who could be carrying his only child. Camille took his dick with force and inserted it inside of her. Their rhythm together was perfect as he pounded deep inside her. For her to be so small she took it like a champ as he bucked her body against his.

The pulsating feeling between my thighs became so intense that secretion of my juices began to escape and trickle down the side. I backed away from the room and stumbled. I turned around and was face to face with Shelly. I was so caught up with the show in front of me that I didn't notice her disappear from the room. She had a devilish grin painted across her face. I froze. I was so embarrassed. She directed her attention to the wet spot that appeared on my light pink pants and licked her lips exposing the tongue ring. She moved in closer to me, so close that her erect nipples were practically stabbing me in my own breast.

"You like what you see Miss Sasha? Would you like a closer look…I won't bite, unless you would like me too," she whispered, hr breath hot on my lips.

My heart began to beat triple time. I was in the most uncomfortable and confusing situation I could ever recall. This was far worse than the night in Greg's office. Part of me wanted to run away from all of this and another part wanted to go jump in that bed and let them have their way.

Shelly backed away smiling, motioning for me to follow her. I watched her move seductively towards the bedroom. By this time Greg had Camille spread eagle and fucked her missionary style on the bed. Shelly went over and sat on

Camille's face for another round of tongue lashing. I was immediately turned on. I couldn't help it; I slid my fingers down my pants and began to finger fuck myself. Soft moans escaped my lips, as I closed my eyes imagining that I was a part of the festivities. Moments later, an eruption occurred from my chasm drenching my panties with hot sticky fluid. My legs buckled causing me to grab a hold of the door for support. I couldn't believe I had an orgasm.

I opened my eyes, only to find Lorenz standing in front of me with his nostrils flared.

"I'm sorry." I was ashamed.

He pushed passed me, "Why Sasha is this the life you want? You want this… Is this what you really want?"

At the sound of Lorenz's voice all activity came to a halt. All the attention was now on us. I walked in pleading.

"No, I want you! I don't know what came over me, baby. I just… I don't know I'm so sorry…It won't happen again…I just want to leave. I…I want us to go home, right now tonight." I begged. I didn't know what to say. I was caught in the act of lust, adultery.

He stood before me with tears in his eyes.

I reached out for his hand. He didn't budge.

"Sasha, how long were you here...watching? Please don't lie?"

"I don't know…I was looking for you."

He cocked his head to the side in disbelief, "You…were looking for *me*…in here...Why…What made you think I would be in here with them? That's not adding up Sash come on now...you really thought I was in here...Do you think I really want these bitches? Do you!"

He wasn't his self at all. His facial expressions changed like one of a mad man.

"You want a show Sash? Is that it? You want me to fuck one of these bitches for you…huh is that it…I guess I got to do this for you then Sasha, this is what *you* want...I guess this is the type of shit that turns you on…huh?"

What was he talking about?

He dropped his pajama pants exposing his erection. He grabbed Shelly by the hair pulling her off the bed. Shelly took her position on her knees as he held her hair and shoved his dick down her throat. Camille and Greg both stood beaming with satisfaction.

He thrust his pelvis slamming against Shelly's face as she devoured my husband's dick.

His voice cracked, “Are you happy now?” He said looking at Greg.

I tried to run out the room but Greg grabbed my arms and pulled me closer as I watched Shelly pleasure my husband. I looked into Lorenz's eyes. He was not enjoying this at all. He was hurting, something wasn't right. I thought about the discussion I overheard in the office earlier...I knew then that this was Greg's doing.

I couldn't take it any longer I broke from his grip and pushed Shelly off my husband. I don't know what I would prove by doing this but I felt it had to be done. I undressed in the middle of the room and grabbed Lorenz's hand pulling him on top of me as I lay on the bed.

The smile faded from Greg's face as he witnessed what was about to go down.

I whispered in my husband's ear.” I know this is not your fault…I want you to fuck me…now.”

I know it was twisted and didn't make much sense, none of this did, we fucked right there on Greg's bed, and put on our own show. I was now free.

Chapter 15

I couldn't believe that March was here already. I was in the mid stages of my pregnancy. Things were going great. Lorenz and I were closer than ever.

Greg had backed off some since the New Years Eve incident. He still tried to control everything that had to do with the baby. He had me change my doctor, and he was there for my first ultra sound. The baby was healthy, but they couldn't determine the gender. No one knew that I was married, and Greg still didn't know that Lorenz knew I was pregnant.

The same went for Lorenz. It was easy to hide. I was five months and still not even showing. He said I was carrying it in my tits. We laughed about it all the time. I had to admit I did go up a bra size. Greg wasn't around often; he had received an award, and spent a lot of time traveling to universities lecturing. I was happy he was away because that gave me time to think about how I was going to get out of my situation.

I still had no idea who the father was. The only way to find out was through DNA testing. This was out of the question, unless I confessed to Lorenz about sleeping with his brother. I was in a no win situation. I know I said I would come clean with him once we were home. But things were going so good, I couldn't bring myself to come out and tell him I was fucking his brother, and this may not be his child.

My feet were killing me. I had been in line for over a half an hour waiting to get a new key. Greg had set me up with a

P.O. Box so I could receive all my mail from North Carolina. He had everything planned out perfectly. I even had a separate bank account for the baby and me. I had to admit, he was looking out for us.

Last month, I decided to go check things out down in Durham. I gave Lorenz some lame excuse about having to go to some conference. He didn't make a fuss. He had been busy preparing for his graduation in May. I think he needed some time to himself.

When I informed Greg that I needed him to cover for me while I took the trip, he was ecstatic. He thought I was finally buying into his dream. He paid for my hotel and airfare. I didn't need him to, but he insisted. I told him I wanted to see the house, and check out the University and the hospital. He made the proper phone calls and I was on my way.

Everything checked out fine. I really did have a job lined up. I met with the chief of staff, and he told me how Gregory spoke highly of me and my resume and credentials were impressive. He couldn't wait to have me on board. I was curious how he would hire me without even talking to me. He said my work spoke for itself, and that Greg had developed some of the best psychologists in the business. I bet after all the mental anguish he's putting me through, it's no wonder I wasn't laying on someone's chair spilling my guts. I met with my future staff members, who were great people. I guess it's true about southerners, they are very hospitable.

The next day I went to visit the campus, which was huge! I spoke with a few professors, who even let me sit in on some of the classes. I was really impressed.

My last stop on my North Carolina tour was to my new home. It was located in Chapel Hill, in a development called Silver Creek; the houses that were complete were beautiful. I thought Greg and Camille's house was breath taking, their house looked like my little starter home compared to this.

The taxi stopped in front of my new house, 3207 San Sophia Drive. Words couldn't explain what was before me.

This house has to cost a fortune.

I got out the car and walked up the drive way. I was greeted by a young gentleman in his mid 20's. He was handsome, dressed in a sharp Ralph Lauren Navy pinstriped suit. He also looked vaguely familiar.

"Are you Ms. Jones?" I couldn't open my mouth to speak. I was still in awe over the house. "Hi, my name is James Duncan. I am one of Dr. Hayward's attorneys. He asked me to show you around and to answer any questions you need answered." He smiled and helped me to the door. "Ma'am, I am aware of your condition and I need you to watch your step." He said with a southern drawl.

Mr. Duncan showed me around the house. It had 4 bedrooms, 4 bathrooms, kitchen, sun room, finished basement with an exercise room, a two story family room, dining room, laundry room, an office, a three car garage, a huge backyard, and deck; it was all I could ever dream of. Greg really outdid himself. It was perfect.

When I returned back from my tour I told him I was not going to put up a fight. That I would go to North Carolina like he wanted. He was so happy. He said he would give me time to break things off with Lorenz. Of course I wasn't going to leave my husband. I just wanted him to believe that. I had to figure out how I could tell Lorenz what was going on and still hold our family together. I didn't want to lose him. But, at the same time I couldn't resist starting over in Chapel Hill. I was determined to make the two work together somehow....

After the long wait, I finally received my key. I opened the box and found what looks like an invitation. I opened it. It was a note from Greg of course, telling me to meet him at our old spot tonight at 10p.m. I sighed.

Here we go again, I thought.

I crumbled up the note and threw it in the trash on my way out the building.

Chapter 16

"Baby...?"

His truck was in the garage, but he didn't answer. I checked the house and he was nowhere to be found.

Where could he be without his truck?

I sat on the bed to call his cell. That's when I noticed the note on the table.

"*Sasha...I went to Wilmington to fill in. I'll call you when I get a free moment. I will see you in the morning.*
I love you."

He must have caught the shuttle. That was a relief; at least I don't have to lie about where I was going at 10p.m. He wouldn't even know I left. I set my alarm for 8:30p.m. I needed to get some rest if I had to deal with Greg, who knows what he had in store....

At 9:45p.m. I pulled in the Embassy parking lot. I dreaded having to go in there. I sat in my car until 10p.m. before I made my way into the hotel. I asked the desk clerk for Dr. Hayward's room.

He asked, "Are you Ms. Jones?"

I wanted to say no, I'm Mrs. Hayward. I showed him my ID, and he gave me a key. I took the elevator to the 6th floor. Room 602, well at least I didn't have far to walk. I opened the door and walked back towards the bedroom area.

"Greg, I'm here." I opened the bedroom door.

"What the fuck is she doing here?" Greg and Lorenz were both there.

"Sasha, what are you doing here?" he turned to Greg, "I thought you said Shelly was coming."

"Shelly? You are here to be with Shelly?"

He came in my face and shouted, "WHAT THE FUCK ARE YOU DOING HERE! WHAT YOU CAME TO FUCK MY BROTHER!"

I looked at Greg he was enjoying all of this. He was smiling his ass off. I couldn't take it...this was too much. I felt my knees getting weak. I was about to buckle. Greg hurried to my side to catch me. Lorenz pushed him out the way.

"GET YOUR FUCKING HANDS OFF MY WIFE!"

"No...No shut up baby…no!" I tried to caution him but it was too late. The shit was about to hit the fan. It was too late.
He lunged at Greg's face who was flabbergasted by what he had heard.

"So I guess you were just going to try and fuck my pregnant wife." He pushed him forcefully.

Greg stood there like a statue speechless.

A demonic look was in his eyes. I never saw nothing like it. He was outraged. Suddenly he pushed Lorenz so hard he went crashing into the entertainment cabinet.

He was coming towards me. I tried to get up but it was too late. He wrapped his hands around my throat.

"Greg...Stop." I pleaded. I was choking.

"You won't leave me again! I won't allow it! You hear me Rachael! I won't allow it!"

Rachael...I'm not Rachael?

My mother's name was Rachael, but why would Dr. Hayward be calling my mother's name. I felt myself getting light headed.

"Greg, the baby...you're hurting the baby!"

He backed off. I began coughing trying to catch my breath and scooted away from him quickly. Lorenz limped over to make sure I was Ok. There was blood leaking from a gash in his head.

"I'm sorry baby...Are you Ok?"

He was crying. "Y-yes…"

"Sash I need you to get out of here." He helped me up and rushed me to the door.

"No...I can't leave you. He'll kill you!"

Greg grabbed him and tried to pull him away from me.

"Sasha run!"

I ran out the door and hopped on the elevator. I hurried out of the building into my car. It had begun to rain heavily. My mind was racing. So much had just happened that I didn't understand. Where did my mother fit into all of this?

Did Greg know her? And if so how? She died when I was young. I never heard anything about Greg Hayward....

As I was getting on the highway I noticed someone speeding up behind me blinding me with their high beams. I tried to get away from him. It was raining and I already couldn't see. This was dangerous, but I had to do it. I dipped between two tractor trailers to get in the far left lane. It was close, but I made it. I was praying that he wouldn't try to do the same. I didn't see him anymore.

I took the scenic route home. When I arrived I locked all my doors, windows and set the alarm. I tried to call Lorenz's cell, but couldn't get through. I tried to make sense of what was happening. It wasn't adding up. What was really going on? Were they both playing with me, if so why? Where did my mother fit into all of this? Maybe he wasn't referring to my mother. My head pounded from all of the thoughts dancing around in my head. Hours had passed before I received a phone call.

Ring...Ring ...I jumped up and answered the phone.

"Lorenz!"

"No...Sasha it's me...Camille."

I didn't recognize her voice. "There's been an accident...."

"Oh God is it Lorenz!" I cried "Where are you?"

"We're at Crozier Trauma Center...you need to calm down. Besides a few scrapes and bruises, Lorenz is fine...but...but," Her voice started cracking, "Greggy didn't make it...."

I dropped the phone in disbelief. I didn't want Greg to die. Not like this. There were too many questions that weren't answered. How would I ever know if he was actually the father?

Chapter 17

After I received the phone call from Camille I immediately began to have severe abdominal pain. I tried to pull myself together so I could get to the hospital but it didn't work. I ended up calling the ambulance for myself.

At the hospital, I was checked out and told I was having a daughter and it was nothing more than shock. That I needed to be on bed rest and remain calm. To be sure that I obeyed their instructions they kept me in the hospital for three days.

Lorenz was back and forth between the hospital and Camille's. We never really had a chance to discuss why he was in the hotel room with Greg waiting on Shelly, or why Greg was calling me Rachael, or how the accident even happened. I had so many questions that were unanswered.

The day of Greg's funeral, he didn't want me to attend. He thought it would be too much stress for me. I told him I was going, he was my boss. How would it look to my co-workers if I didn't show up? He didn't want to argue. So he took my keys so I wouldn't be able to go. I let him think that he'd won. I had another set hidden in my garage. I was going to this funeral. I owed it to my baby.

When I arrived at St. Paul's AME Church I couldn't find a parking space. There were police directing traffic because the roads were blocked. It was total chaos. I had to park two blocks away from the church. When I entered the building it was packed. There was no more room in the sanctuary so the ushers were trying to seat me in the overflow.

"Ma'am Greg was my boss and brother in law…I need to be seated inside."

She rolled her eyes, "Ma'am, if you are kin, why didn't you ride with the family? I'm sorry, you have to go to the other room, there's no room in the sanctuary."

I didn't want to make a scene so I headed to the back with the other mourners. I felt a tug at my arm, it was Starla. She was dressed in this cute little black Dior dress.

"Hey Sasha, follow me. I can get you a seat, but it won't be with the family, there's just not enough room. Oh and there's no viewing either…Daddy had something written up in his will about not being viewed." She shrugged her shoulders.

She opened the doors to the sanctuary and it was beyond packed. You would have thought it was a celebrities home going.

"Please don't tell your uncle I'm here."

She nodded and headed towards the front. I looked around and saw many familiar faces. I spotted his colleagues from Duke, and all of the hospital staff. Even a few of his patients had come. They had a picture of Greg next to his flower adorned mahogany casket. I cried. I didn't want it to end this way. I should have been stronger. I should have never allowed that to happen in his office. I was crying harder now.

One of the ushers came up to ask if I was alright. She must have noticed I was pregnant so she was concerned. They were about to read his eulogy. I forgot to get a program. I listened as the speaker began.

"We are here this afternoon to pay tribute to a great man, Dr. Lorenz Gregory Hayward, Sr."

Did he just say Lorenz?

He continued on, "Dr. Hayward leaves behind his loving wife, Camille D. Conners-Hayward, step daughter, Starla Rayne Conners, and beloved son Lorenz Gregory Hayward Jr."

"Son!" I said out loud. The people around me turned to look.

*Did he say so*n?

I was going to be sick; I ran out the sanctuary to the

bathroom and began to vomit. I sat in the stall crying.

I'm fucking stupid! His father! I was fucking his son! This may be my husband's sister I am carrying, or Greg's grand-daughter.

I kicked the stall door and screamed. Why is this happening to me? My head was spinning everything was coming to my mind. That's why Lorenz was so loyal to Greg, he was his dad.

"Sasha...open the door." The familiar voice said, "Open the door now!" I opened the door and there was Camille.

"Get up!" Her voice was cold, "Don't cry now Miss Sasha, it's too late! I know you were fucking my husband, and I know you're carrying his baby."

She helped me up from the floor and handed me a tissue. I couldn't look at her; I was too ashamed.

"I don't know if I want to hug you or slap you. You remind me so much of your mother."

That got my attention.

"How do you know my mother?" I snapped.

"Wow...so you really are in the dark." She locked the bathroom door, "Take a seat sweetie, we need to talk."

Chapter 18

"Miss Sasha where should I begin...." Camille kicked off her heels and sat next to me on the cream lounge chair in the bathroom.

"About 31 years ago my Greggy and your mother...Rachael use to be an item, well at least he thought. The thing is your mom was in love with your father, Mixxon, "Big Mixx". By the way, he's not in Panama, nor is he from there. Your father is a Dominican Kingpin, or at least he was, until he caught a murder charge! Last I heard, he was doing a life sentence in Smyrna Correctional Facility."

"In Delaware?"

"Yeah, that one...But don't interrupt me...let me tell you all the details then you can ask questions later. Greggy and Big Mixx were tight, they used to hustle together. Yeah...honey Greggy had a past. Long story short, Mixx caught a petty charge and had to do eighteen months in the FEDS, so Greg promised to look out for your mom, until Mixx got home." She said taking a breath to continue, "Greg had a girlfriend named Becca, who was Renzo's mom. Becca loved Greg to death and I mean literally to death. Greg and your mother started spending a lot of time together and one thing led to another and they started creeping. Rachael told Greg she was pregnant. Greg being naive automatically thought it was his. He didn't know Rachael was already four months pregnant. Greg started getting into Rachael, and spending less time with Becca." She paused, "A few months later, Becca ends up pregnant. Greg wasn't too happy about that. He had fallen in love with your mom, but your mom was playing Greg big time. She was all about the money. She just wanted someone to take care of her while her man was doing a bid. Greg told Becca to have an abortion because he and Rachael were about to have a baby girl. Becca was vexed. She tried to tell Greg that Rachael was lying and that it was Mixx's baby! He didn't believe her. He gave Becca abortion money because he thought he was going to be with Rachael." Sighing, "Like three months later, Rachael goes into labor, and had you. She lied to Greg and told him she went into premature labor. He believed it. He never questioned your looks, because you looked exactly like your mother. So he thinks everything is cool. What he didn't know was...not only did Becca not have the abortion, but she wrote Big Mixx, and told him everything! A few months passed and Mixx got out early. Becca felt guilty, because she still loved Greg and wanted to tell him to leave because Mixx was coming to get him. Well, she got there a little too late because Mixx was already at Rachael's making her tell Greg the truth about you not being his child. After the truth was out Mixx pulls a gun on Greg...Becca ran in front of the gun and he shot her three times. So Becca was rushed to the hospital. Greg was right by her side. The doctors informed Becca's mom that they couldn't save both Becca and the baby. Greg begged her to choose Becca. Her mother wanted to know if Becca would be the same if she pulled through. The doctors couldn't give her a definite answer. So her mom chose the baby...And that baby was Lorenz Jr.

Greg was vexed. He was going to get Mixx back for what he had done. Mixx was on the run, but they ended up catching him. Rachael moved to Brookhaven with her sister. Lorenz Jr. went home with Becca's mom until she had a nervous breakdown when he was a year old. Greg's mom stepped in and adopted him and raised them together as brothers. Greg didn't really take to him because he blamed him for Becca's death. He believed that they should have saved her instead. Lorenz didn't find out that Greg was actually his father until his 18th birthday. The sad thing is

Greg never stopped loving Rachael."

"I thought you said he wanted Becca to live...I thought he loved Becca." I was confused.

"He wanted her to live because he felt guilty for not believing her; he didn't want the guilt on him, he couldn't live with the fact that she had given her life for his. He was in love with your mother. He was determined to be with her again, not Becca. Now let me finish...Greg did see your mother again. She found out that she had cancer and she wanted to ask a favor of Greg. Greg and I were married around that time. He told me that she was coming and he needed to see her...I was cool with it; because I wanted to see this infamous Rachael anyway. She came to see the house and brought a picture of you. She apologized to Greg for what she had done. She told him she didn't have long to live and she asked if Greg could look after you. He promised he would."

"They kept in touch until she passed."You went to Padua Academy for high school right?"

"Yes."

"Yeah, she said knowingly. Greg paid for that.

We were at your graduations, both high school and college. What made you want to go into Psychology?" she asked.

I had to think...I really didn't remember...Oh wait a minute. I said, "My mom used to tell me how much she wanted to be one. I used to get different magazines and literature in the mail. I thought it was some type of sign."

She laughed out loud, "Yeah, a sign from Greg. He asked your mother to drill that in you. I guess it was part of his plan to keep you near." She sighed deeply, "Sasha, I am truly sorry that you are finding all this out now. I really am."

I couldn't believe that she was actually being nice. "So is that it?" I asked, "Is this everything I need to know?"

"No Sweetie. That was easy, now the rest is going to be a hard pill for you to swallow…You just wait right here, I have to go back in for a minute before someone comes looking for me." She hopped off the counter and slipped back into her shoes and strutted out the door.

I sat there in total disbelief; so much was happening. I couldn't believe what I was hearing. Greg was in love with my mother. I shook my head in disbelief. If he loved my mother so much, why was he so mean to me? Why was he trying to make me suffer? The whole thought of Greg thinking I was his child sickened me. Why would he want to sleep with someone he once thought was his own daughter? I had more questions. I waited for Camille to come back to the bathroom. She returned fifteen minutes later. She locked the door and handed me a cup of water.

"Is the service almost over?"

"Yeah right! They're letting all of his boring friends make speeches about his accomplishments. The preacher hasn't gotten up yet...We have plenty of time...to chit chat." She pulled a miniature bottle of Jack Daniels from her clutch bag and took a swig.

"Let me warn you...you may not like what you are about to hear...I can't have any outbursts or hysterical cries ok." I nodded.

I mean what could be worse than what I was already hearing?

She went on with her story. "Although Greg promised your mother he would look out for you...He still didn't like the fact that Mixx was your father...or the fact that Mixx tried to kill him. He was going to get him back for what he had done...He figured the best way to get at him was through you...Greg hired you because he had a plan from the beginning, but I'm going to get to that in a minute."

She walked over and hopped on the counter, "Now I know you're wondering where Lorenz comes in the picture...Well he was still in school in Baltimore, trying his hardest to please Greg, bending over backwards for his acceptance. But, see he was never good enough...Not compared to you anyway. Greg would always compare him to you. He never called you by name...He would say yeah be like Rachael's daughter. Lorenz wasn't too thrilled when he found out he made 'Rachael's daughter' his assistant, after he begged Greg for the position.
He wanted to work with his father so they could form a bond.

But, Greg was so into you. Well Lorenz was fed up and needed to know just who this 'Rachael's daughter' was. He had never seen her; he just lived in her shadow. So he started coming by the hospital, trying to find out who you were. He didn't have a name or face so he was going to find out on his own. He didn't know that Greg had more than one female assistant, so he figured Karyn was Rachael's daughter. Especially since Greg was nice to her." Shaking her head, "He directed all his hatred towards Karyn. Then he saw you. I remember how he came home, and was like Camille I think I found my future wife. You know me I wasn't trying to hear that because I wanted him as my own little toy. I went along with him for a while. As time went on he was still talking about this woman. So after about eight months into his obsession, I asked him what her name was... He asked me to promise not to tell Greg. I promised, he said her name was Sasha...Sasha Jones. She's Greg's other assistant. I said to him I thought you hated her. He was like, 'no...Karyn, Karyn is Rachael's daughter'...He went on to say he didn't even see what was so great about Karyn, that you were more qualified, and Greg treated you like shit...." She looked over in my direction.

"Are you ok Sasha?" I lied and said I was, but I wasn't aware my husband hated me, or at least he hated the person he thought was me. My head was hurting.

"Do you want me to go on?"

I told her to continue because I needed to know everything now!

"So I was like damn...he thinks Karyn is Rachael's daughter, and in all actuality, he is jonez'n on Sasha, who is really Rachael's daughter. I wanted to tell him; look, you need to back off because you're in for the shock of your life. But I didn't, I wanted to see what was going to happen." She giggled, "You know me, I'm down for some good drama. Over the summer that just past, Lorenz put in for an internship at your hospital. He didn't go through Greg; he went through Dr. Wynn. Dr. Wynn told Greg that he accepted his son into the program, and he was placing him with you. That's when I became concerned and told Greg that he was really into you, and wanted to pursue a relationship. That's when Greg told me that he was sleeping with you--"

I cut in.

"That's not true; I wasn't sleeping with him then." Camille rolled her eyes.

"Anyway, like I was saying...he told me ya'll was fucking, but of course I didn't care. I had my own side pieces...I just thought it was kind of sick that he was screwing someone he once thought was his own child...I think everyone in that field of work is a little twisted anyway. So he said that he was telling him that you were Rachael's daughter and he was going to prove to Lorenz and Mixx that you were a conniving slut like your mom."

Again she had lost me. "I thought he loved my mom, why would he call her a slut?"

"I don't know Sasha..." She snapped. "Greg was complicated...he did love her, but he still had resentment in his heart. I mean who wouldn't, she played him, had him open. He really thought they were going to be a family. Then on top of that she had the nerve to come back and ask him to look out for you. She just opened up old wounds again...She should have just stayed away!" Camille was getting angry, "Greg told Lorenz that he needed help to carry out a plan so he could have his revenge on 'Rachael'. Of course he agreed. But see the joke was on him. He didn't expect you to walk through that office door. Lorenz didn't want to believe that you were actually Rachael's daughter and not Karyn. That's when Greg showed him the picture of Rachael, and Lorenz saw that you were a splitting image. He wanted to back out, but it was too late, he had to continue on with the plan.
He didn't want to disappoint his dad. He really started to fall for you and Greg knew it. He still didn't realize that you were already fucking Greg the whole time."

She was getting on my nerves. "I was not--"

She cut me off, "Cut the shit Sasha...You don't have to lie I already know, that ya'll have been fucking for years! I don't care...my GOD! I'm happy that you were...That gave me more time to do me! So, Greg continued to fuck you and send the video's to Mixx of him fucking his daughter."

"He did what!"

"Yeah, you know Greg has connections everywhere. He made sure Mixxon saw the video tapes of him and Lorenz fucking you. So you can kiss that reunion goodbye…I don't think your daddy would want to see you, especially since you and your mother was fucking his arch enemy."

I didn't know what to say. I just felt like dying.

"Now, Miss Sasha...You know the apple don't fall far from the tree. Lorenz is no different than Greg, he is obsessed with you. What do you think he will do when he finds out you are carrying his brother or sister? Do you think he is still going to marry you when he finds out that you were fucking his dad?"

She didn't know the truth.

She pulled an envelope out of her purse. I opened it; there was a cashier's check worth $100,000.00.

"Leave Sasha, save yourself and the baby. You're a smart girl, you can start over."

She looked down at my ring.

"Hmm...If you know like I know I would take that Melee Brilliant and get what I could get for it."

This was all too much for me to handle.

"Why are you doing all this for me?"

She laughed, "It's not for you it's for me..."

She pulled out another envelope.

"Sign this please."

It was a letter stating that I wouldn't put Greg's name on the birth certificate or try to claim any monies later in life for the baby. I should have known. She was trying to pay me off. I took the papers and I signed them. I wanted to be done with all of them.

She smiled in satisfaction. "You did the right thing honey."

She wouldn't be saying that if she knew what I had awaiting me in North Carolina...and that's exactly where I was headed.

Chapter 19

As I drove home I tried to make sense of everything that occurred over the last few years. I was astonished that Greg was the foundation of who I had become. I couldn't believe how much power one man had over so many people's lives.

My husband. The thought of his betrayal was killing me. I had mixed emotions about our relationship. I wanted to believe that he really loved me and wanted to build a family. But how could you build a family on treachery. I couldn't trust him. I thought about my father, Mixxon. I wondered what he thought of me. I couldn't believe that Greg sent him video's of me fucking him. I really couldn't get over the fact that Lorenz continued to video tape us. Was he that desperate for Greg's approval? I know that had to tear him apart.

My mother, that really caught me off guard. I guess I am like her in more ways than one. She was all about herself. Why would she go back to Greg after what she had done to him? This is all her fault. My life is in shambles because of her being selfish. Tears started to stream. Hate was being formed against my dead mother.

Camille, Camille...Camille...She thought she was so slick. She had me sign my child's so called inheritance away. She's so stupid. I managed a small snicker. If only she knew, my baby was already financially secure. I guess Greg didn't tell her everything, or she would have known about the house in my name, which was paid for. I guess he didn't mention the trust fund, or the plush job he had set up for me. She had the audacity to throw $100,000.00 at me to keep his name off the birth certificate. Little did she know his name was never going on it? My husband would be named as my little girls' father.

My thoughts were interrupted by the phone ringing.

"Hello."

It was him. He had called to tell me that Camille really broke down at the burial and he was going to stay at the house tonight to make sure she didn't do anything harmful to herself. Camille had followed through with the plan. I told him that it was cool, and I would talk to him later. He told me he loved me, and my heart felt as if it had been stung by a scorpion.

"I love you too...I *really* loved you, always remember that." I said.

He told me he would see me in the morning and hung up. I hung up the phone and shook my head. It would be many mornings before he saw my face again.

I rushed in the house and started to pack my things. I made sure I had all my important documents, laptop, anything that would be of value to me. I called a locksmith and told them I needed to change my locks. They told me no one could come out for a few hours. I begged and pleaded for them to send someone. I told them I had an ex who was abusive and I was pregnant. They were here in like ten minutes. The guy even helped me load my car.

I took most of his belongings and sat them on the deck. All his important paper work I was dropping off at the hospital. I called a moving company and asked how much they would charge to have my house packed and ready to move within 24 hours. Of course they tried to say it was impossible, but everyone knows money talks. I threw a few numbers at them and about an hour or two later I had a crew packing my house. I gave them the keys, and my new address to where my things were going. I looked at my house one more time before leaving and drove to begin phase two of my getaway plan.

I stopped by the hospital to drop off his things. I went to my office and emailed human resources and told them I was taking a leave. Greg had already informed them of my pregnancy and that I was not coming back, that I was becoming a stay at home mom. They had no idea who the father was. Greg told them I wanted my own privacy so they didn't ever mention it to anyone, including me.

I packed up my things and headed out. I was happy no one was there, because I didn't want to answer any questions. My next stop was the bank. I withdrew all of my savings. My last stop was the police station. I filed a PFA against Lorenz. I told them I was pregnant and he threatened me, and I was afraid he was going to do something. Of course they fell for it and signed an order. I thanked them and left. I then faxed the order to the moving company so if he happened to stop by the house before they were gone he couldn't get in. I didn't feel a bit of regret for what I had done. After all that was done to me I had the right to be a little vindictive.

Camille told me she would put my house up for sale and send me the papers that needed to be signed along with my check. I told her not to worry about it. I didn't want her to know where I was going. She thought I was starting over out west. I turned my car's navigational system on, I read...7 hours before I would be totally free.

On the way, I had to get some rest. So I stopped at a hotel. Listening to the radio in my room I heard, *"I wish I had known that you'd come for me I was a soul that was lost and incomplete. You were my friend, now you're my man and I want you always I, I just don't know what came over me, boy you touched my soul and let me feel free. Always be there, and baby don't be scared cause I'll love ya always Baby always....."*

I sobbed quietly to myself. That was our song. I was lying on the bed listening to the quiet storm on the radio. I turned the radio off and walked over to the window. It had started to rain. I had become skeptical of my decision of leaving. My heart was aching. I missed Lorenz. I sat at the window reminiscing over the good times we shared.

Then Camille's words rang in my head.

'He hated Rachael's daughter... he was tired of living in

her shadow...The apple doesn't fall far from the tree...'

I sighed. I was certain that I had done the right thing. I shut the curtains and returned to the bed. I was in Richmond, VA. Tomorrow I would get back on the road to continue my journey to Chapel Hill.

Onto I-95 South, I checked my said seven hours until destination...*the end to my beginning…*

Chapter 20

Camille

"Oh my God, Greggy. Oh Lawd...Why you take my husband...," I cried.

I had to put on a show we still had company in the house. Lorenz sat next to me holding me in his arms. He was right where I wanted him. I buried my head in his chest.

"Greggy...Greggy...Why you leave me...Oh God...My Greggy is gone..." I looked up helplessly at him, "What am I going to do Renzo? My Greggy is gone. I have nothing... NOTHING!"

He had so much compassion in his eyes. He was really buying into my theatrics. I stood up...I began to wobble, took a few steps, and hit the floor. Lorenz and another young man ran over to get me up. All eyes were on me. I made my body limp as if I had passed out. I heard him say he was going to carry me to my room. I heard people whispering as he carried me up the stairs. They were all falling for it. They thought I really gave a shit about dead ass Greg! I was happy the son of a bitch was gone...I was finally free. No more having to hear about fat ass Sasha and her dead bitch of a mom. I can't believe she really thought I was going to let her bastard ass child get what belonged to me. She must have bumped her head.

He laid me on the bed and I opened my eyes. "Please don't leave...I'm scared, I can't be alone," I whimpered.

He told me he needed to call Sasha and let her know he was

staying. I laid there acting as if I was in distress. She should be long gone by now I thought. This was working out better than I thought it would. I had managed to make her believe that he really hated her.

Truth is his dumb ass would have accepted that baby, because he was just as stuck on her as Greg was Rachael. He would have looked right past the fact that she had been screwing his father. But I refused to let them win. They had my husband's mind all screwed up for years. I had to look elsewhere for affection. Different men and women had shown me more love than my own husband. I even got more affection from Lorenz than I did Greg. I deserve to be happy. I deserved so much more than this. I was determined to get it.

Later that night...

"Greg...Greggy is that you?" I walked into Lorenz's room ass naked. "You came back to me..." I ran to the bed. He grabbed me.

"No, Camille it's me, Lorenz...Greg is dead. He's gone."

I kept on with my game. I rubbed my naked flesh against him. I grabbed his face and began to suck his lips.

"Greggy...I...Can't believe it's you." I said in between kisses. He tried to gently push me away.

"No, Camille it's me, stop."

I began to kiss on his nipples and grab at his dick that was beginning to swell. He wanted me. I knew he did. Next thing I know...I felt his hand slap across my face. I fell to the floor. He came over to me.

"Oh my God, Camille, I'm so sorry. I didn't mean to hit you."

He held me in his strong arms apologizing. That was my chance to take what I wanted. I glanced up at him and conjured up a few fake tears.

"Please Greggy, I need to feel you in me one more time...I need you to make me feel good one more time." I stroked his manhood and nibbled on his chest. "Please, take me one... more...time."

He held me tightly looking toward the ceiling. This

situation had him jammed. I had him in the palm of my hands. He played along.

"One more time...and then Greggy has to go." He weakly whispered.

He rose to his feet, gently lifted me off the floor and carried me to my room where we had hot passionate sex. Greg was right Lorenz was weak. He played right into me. I had him right where I wanted him. And once he finds out that Sasha left him, he would be mine.

Sasha

I arose at 7:30 in the morning. After I showered and dressed. I thought about calling him, but I chose not to. I would be hearing from him later today for sure. I went downstairs for the complimentary breakfast, and then got back on the road.

At 12:30p.m. I had finally arrived in Durham, NC. I was relieved. I stopped at the gas station to get directions to the nearest hotel. The attendant told me there was a Double Tree not far from Hillsboro Street, which was about ten minutes away. I thanked him and got back in the car. I heard a beeping noise coming from my cell phone; it said I had one missed call. I checked the number and it was Lorenz. I turned the phone off and put it back in my purse. I couldn't talk to him. I wasn't ready.

Now what do I do?

I finished unpacking my things and put them away. I thought about calling him, but I wasn't sure what to say. It was going on 2p.m. I know he's been to the house by now. I wonder what his reaction was. I wonder if they were done packing my house before he came. I wonder if Camille told him I knew everything. I grabbed my purse and turned my phone back on. Twenty-five missed calls. Most of them were Lorenz's number, and a few private calls. I knew the private calls were from him too, he just blocked out his number. I called my voice mail, it was full. I couldn't bear to hear what he said so I just erased them all.

Ring! Ring! I was startled, the phone had begun to ring again; I sat it on the bed and watched it for over an hour as it continuously rung.

Finally I had had enough, I took a deep breath, "Hello", I said in a cheerful voice.

"*SASHA! WHAT TYPE OF GAME ARE YOU PLAYING! WHEN DID I EVER ABUSE YOU! TELL ME THAT...WHEN THE FUCK DID I PUT MY HANDS ON YOU...ARE YOU FUCKING* CRAZY!" He was heated.

I remained calm.

"Could you please refrain from using foul language with me… you did put your hands on me. Remember that night at the Hilton, when you pushed my head on the bed and attempted to beat me with a belt." I had caught him off guard with that one.

"*WHAT...THE HILTON...SASHA YOU SENT ME AN EMAIL TALKING ABOUT THAT'S WHAT YOU WANTED...YOU WANTED ME TO HIT YOU...AND...AND HOW YOU GONNA MAKE THOSE TYPES OF ACCUSATIONS WITH NO PROOF...*"

I cut him off, "Proof...I have no proof. No that's where your mistaken I have plenty of proof. Oh, let me rephrase that, my dad, Mixxon has plenty of proof. You made sure of that didn't you?"

There was dead silence on the phone.

"Oh! You ain't got nothing to say now; you awfully quiet...Yeah, I know how you and your DADDY tried to set me up, yeah that's right, it's all out!" I was on a roll now my heart was racing.

"Let me explain Sasha, I didn't mean to...I didn't know you was her daughter, I thought it was Karyn. You have to believe me. I never wanted to hurt you...I wa--"

"You didn't want to hurt me, then why didn't you just tell the truth…."

Silence.

"Do you know how I felt, when I heard them announce you were Greg's son? Do you know how I feel knowing that you knew so much about my father, and I knew nothing, nothing at all? You could have told me the truth after we were married. Or was that all in the plans too."

"Sasha..." He began to cry, "You got to believe me. I love

you. I wanted to tell you the truth, but he wouldn't let me...He told me he would hurt you if I tried to tell you, he was going to hurt you..."

I didn't believe a word he was saying, "So now you want to cry...What you crying for Lorenz? It's too late you already dug a hole too deep to pull yourself out of...."

"Wha-What do you mean...I can't pull myself out of. You're my wife and you have my baby. We have to work this out. I need you. I can't live without you...I have no one else. Sasha I will die. I'll die if you leave."

I was feeling bad, but I couldn't fall for it. "It's too late I'm already gone!"

I hung up the phone and cried myself to sleep....

***

Three of the longest days of my life had past. I lounged around the hotel room contemplating on how I would handle my next confrontation with Lorenz. I hadn't heard from him since our last conversation. Believe me it wasn't because he hadn't called. Truth is I turned my cell off to avoid him. I was still having mixed emotions about the situation. I wanted to stay angry and hate him, but deep inside I am still weak for him. I couldn't lie, I loved that man. But I had to put my feelings aside for a moment. I had to make sure he was really in love with me or if it was all a part of the game his father and he were playing. I had accomplished a few things over the course of the days. I had managed to have my OB/GYN switched. I found my way to the Department of Motor Vehicles and had my license and car tags switched. The DMV clerk tried to give me a hard time about my address. She said I had to be living in my house before I could actually prove residence. I thought that was the dumbest thing I ever heard. I showed her my deed, and every other document that could've possibly proved that I owned the house and I would be residing in it. She argued me down for about a half an hour about how that didn't prove that I was a resident of North Carolina, especially at that address. After a while I finally figured where she was coming from. She didn't believe I could afford to live in that type of community. I called her on it and she caught an instant attitude and got her manager. Needless to say, ten minutes later I was walking away with my tags, license, and a lengthy apology. I guess some things never change.

Chapter 21

Sasha

This morning I spoke with Mr. Duncan. He was the attorney that showed me around during my last visit. I called him to ask how long it would be before I could move in. To my surprise he said he had been trying to get in touch with me, ever since my father died.

Father ?

I didn't even question it. I decided to wait until our meeting to find out what he was talking about. When Mr. Duncan arrived, he was dressed in a dark blue designer suit. He wore a pair of stunna shades. I had to laugh, his ass was most definitely country. He was blinging everywhere. This was a big difference in his appearance from the last time. He must have read my mind.

"After I leave here, I am going to hang out with my Frat brothers." He explained.

I laughed, "Oh, it's Ok...It's just a big change from the last time I saw you, that's all.

Damn he's hot.

I led him to the little wooden table. He opened up his briefcase and pulled out a stack of papers. He pulled out a pair of designer glasses and put them on. He was ready to get down to business.

"I want to give you my condolence. Your father was a good man. I had great respect for him and was honored to handle his affairs. Your father had several properties that he owned in this area." He explained, "Uhh...It says here that all the properties are to be turned over to Ms. Sasha Jones as guardian until her first born; his grand child reaches the age of 21. All properties except for the three townhouses located in the RTP. He left that for you to do as you please."

I was amazed; he is still shocking me from his grave. But he still wasn't finished.

"There is also a shopping strip that he owns in Charlotte. That is also willed to the child, and you are to handle it until he or she turns 21."

This was all too much for me at once. Well...At least I know where all this money was coming from.

"What about his wife and son? You are aware that I'm not really his daughter."

For some reason he didn't look surprised.

"I...I already kind of figured that out...I mean you look nothing like him. As for his wife and son, they have no knowledge of any of this existing and he wanted it to stay that way. Dr. Hayward knew Camille was out for his money. She had no idea of what he had accomplished on this end. We made sure everything was tightly secure and had no loopholes so in case Camille tries to dig, or Lorenz Jr., they couldn't put any claims on these properties."

Maybe Greg wasn't as bad as I thought.

He continued to go through the paper work. I signed everything after reading it.

"When do you think I'll be able to move in the house? Is it near completion?"

"Mid-April, is what they say…I can see if they can put a rush on things if you need to be in there sooner. Ms. Jones, why don't you just stay in one of the houses or apartments until it's finished?"

"Is there any vacancies in the apartments? I really don't want anything big being as though my stay would be temporary."

He gathered the papers and placed them in his briefcase.

"How about I pick you up tomorrow around noon, and we'll go check it out. That way you can make your own choice. As a matter of fact, I'll show you all the properties and when you're up to it, we can take a trip to Charlotte to check out the strip mall. You have a lot of work ahead of you and in the condition you're in, you may want to hire someone to oversee these projects for you...Hint...Hint." He winked as he made his way to the door.

"So how about tomorrow?"

"Oh...Yeah tomorrow…that would be great."

"See you then."'"

After Mr. Duncan left I laid across the bed trying to make sense of it all, thoughts of Lorenz clouded my mind. I was curious about how he was holding up. I sat on the bed and turned my cell on. Once again, my message box was full. I started going through and deleting them. There was one message from Camille.

"Sasha, I need you to call me, immediately! Seriously, I need to hear from you like yesterday!"

I checked the time and date, it was left last night. I wasn't sure if I wanted to call; especially after learning about all the properties Greg had. I wondered if somehow she found out about it. I took a deep breath, and called her cell. I didn't want to call the house in case Lorenz answered. She answered on the first ring.

"Sasha! Is that you?"

"Yeah, what's up Camille? Is everything cool?" I tried to play it off.

"Is everything *coo*l? What the hell do you think?" She wasn't too happy.

"Lorenz is losing his damn mind! He's not eating; he's refusing to go back to work. Hell, he's even talking about not going to his graduation! You need to fix this… Now!"

I was confused.

"Fix what Camille? You are the one who told me to leave because he would snap out when he found out about the baby!" Camille began to speak in a hush tone.

"Yeah...but that was before I found out you were *married* already!"

She got me on that one; I should have known she would find out sooner or later.

"Yeah, Miss Sasha, I guess you had your little secrets too. He is sitting here talking about not being able to live without his *wife*, and he wants to see *his* child born, *his* baby, matter of fact he said his *daughter*...So, I am going to be a step grandmother or is it my step daughter? "

Damn it. I was speechless.

"I can't hear ya Sasha...you say something? Oh yeah that's right you don't know what to say because you have been playing games too I see...So you listen to me. You call your *husband* and fix this; I don't care what you tell him, but you better fix this. I refuse to let you ruin another man in this family."

"I thought you said that he didn't care," my voice was weakening, "I thought you said he was going to hate me, when he found--"

She cut me off, "That's before I knew he thought his damn unborn sister was his child. Or it may be his, who knows with your nasty ass! You turned out to be worse than your mother! You better fix this shit, some way! Or I will!"

She slammed the phone down.

I held the phone crying. I hated her. I wasn't ready for him to know where I was. I damn sure didn't want her to tell him the truth about everything. I had to fix this, I didn't know how, but I had to do this before Camille became more involved. I wiped my face and called his cell...he answered. He sounded as if he was worse off than some of our patients.

"Sasha...Baby please, where are you? I need you Sasha." He pleaded.

"I can't tell you where I am right now, but I promise you I will keep in touch, and I will answer your calls, but you have to give me some time to heal."

"Sasha...you don't understand how I feel, right now...I can't go on...I need you...I need to be there when my baby is born, I need my family. You're all I got."

"I understand that sweetheart, but you have to do this my way, and you have to promise to continue on with your life, as if this didn't happen. I mean I am still your wife there is only so much I can do...and I am carrying *your* daughter. I promise if you can do this my way, you will be here for her birth."

It was killing me to hear him that way. It was hard to hold back tears. He was really torn apart. But I still wasn't ready to forgive and forget. I was just getting Camille off my back until I could figure out why she was so concerned about Lorenz.

The next morning when I woke up I noticed that my legs were swollen. They looked as if they were water balloons. I poked my finger in my leg, and it left a dent. It had never done that before. I wasn't sure if I should call my doctor or not. I stuck my finger in another part and it did it again. I didn't feel funny; I was just a little tired. But that's normal; I was now seven months pregnant. I decided that it was nothing and went to get ready for my outing with Mr. Duncan.

At 11:30 there was a knock at my door. I answered and Mr. Duncan was standing there looking awfully fine. He had on a pair of Roca Wear jeans, with a matching Polo shirt. On his feet he sported a pair of fresh white Air Ones. I wanted to change my outfit. I felt a bit unfashionable compared to him. I had on a baby doll maternity shirt, a pair of maternity jeans, and Keds. I definitely looked like someone's mother.

"Are you ready?"

"Yes, just one minute. Let me grab my purse."

He held the door open for me as I walked out. I noticed him checking me out in the elevator. I was embarrassed. I mean this man was fine, and here I was looking a mess. As we were exiting the lobby he asked me to wait for him to get the car.

"How about you wait here for me while I go get the car." He didn't want me to have to walk a long distance.

Damn...Was it that noticeable that I was out of breath? I had picked up a few extra pounds and today I just seemed to be dragging.

He pulled up a few minutes later in a black on black Nissan Maxima. I thought he would have had a Benz or BMW. I mean nothing was wrong with the car. It was hot, fully loaded, and it had to be the latest model out.

He got out and opened the door for me as he said, "Take your time." He helped me in the car, and shut my door.

"You know you didn't have to help me in the car."

He gave me a hesitant look, "I was just trying to help you out; you don't look to well today. I didn't mean to offend you."

"Oh...no, I just didn't want you to think I'm helpless. I mean you're being so nice."

He patted my hand. "I'm just doing what any man would do for a lady as lovely as you."

I couldn't help it. I began to blush.

"I can't figure out why any man would have you doing this by yourself… you know; leaving you alone and pregnant."

He didn't look my way he kept driving. I listened to him speak, trying to see where he was coming from. So far he seemed sincere.

"Well, actually I left him. I have a lot going on right now, and our situation is complicated and I need time alone to sort things out."

I hoped that would have stopped him from trying to dig any further.

"Mr. Duncan, are you married?"

He grinned. *Nice smile.*

"No, and you can call me Jay. My father is Mr. Duncan. I'm married to my job...until God sends me my angel." He made eye contact with me and winked.

The look he gave me, made me nervous. I played it off ignoring his last comment.

"Yeah, I know that feeling. My job consumed me too."

He laughed.

"It didn't consume you too much; you managed to get a bun in the oven."

I smiled. *If only he knew what my job consumed of.*

We made a right onto Waterford Valley Drive.

"We are here."

He pulled up in the parking lot. I was checking out the scenery. I was confused. This was not what I expected to see when he said apartments. This was an actual apartment complex. There were three buildings with patios and balconies, even a rental office. This had to be wrong. I know Greg didn't have this type of money. *How could he have hidden it from Camille?* He opened the car door for me, and we walked to the rental office.

"The office closes at 12p.m. on Saturday's, but I have the keys...You already have a full staff hired. Mrs. Claire Daniel's is the manager. She is aware that you are now the owner of R.S Jones Enterprises."

"R.S. Jones Enterprises? What's that?"

"Ms. Jones did you read anything that you signed? That's the name Dr. Hayward does business under."

"I...I must have not paid any attention." I was baffled.

R.S Jones...Oh...my God...Rachael Sandra Jones, he named his company after my mom.

A sickening feeling came over me. I sat on the bench outside the office trying to get myself together. Jay sat next to me.

"Sasha. Are you Ok? Do you want to do this another time?"

"Oh no...I'm fine I just needed to sit for a moment."

He wore an uneasy look. He held my hand as I took slow deep breaths. I felt a slight panic attack arising. This was all too much for me; there was so much about my mother I didn't know. I'm unsure if her sins from the past where going to be a blessing for me or a curse.

Chapter 22

We road pass the townhouses and checked them out. They were all occupied so we just drove by them so I could at least know where they were located. Greg really had his business in order.

Now I know where all his drug money went.

On our way back to the hotel he asked me if I was hungry. I told him yes. We stopped by Applebee's for a late lunch. Once inside we were seated at a booth.

"Are you sure you'll be comfortable sitting here? I don't want to hurt the baby."

I smiled, "Yes, I'll be fine. I'm not that big am I?"

"No...No...Not at all, as a matter of fact, you're just like I like them, nice and thick. I'm from the South we love thickness."

I was blushing again.

While we were ordering our food my cell phone rang...it was Lorenz. I asked Jay to excuse me, and I answered the phone.

"Hello..."

"Hey Honey. How are you and my little girl doing today?" He was cheerful.

"We are fine, I am just a little tired...could...well...do you mind if...I give you a call back a little later. I'm kind of in the middle of lunch."

Just then the waiter shows up to bring Jay his drink. "Here you are Sir, can I get you anything else?"

Jay replied, "No I'm fine…Sasha, do you need anything?"

"No, I'm good."

I was hoping he wouldn't hear him, but with my luck he did.

"Sasha, who is that in the background? Are you out on a date?" I could hear the anger flaring up in his voice. Jay noticed the look on my face.

"Ms. Jones, is everything alright?" I nodded my head.

"Umm, Sweetie...his name is Mr. Duncan. He is a lawyer who is helping me with my father's business."

"Your father…as in Mixxon Diaz?"

"Yeah, that's right. My father..." I was happy that I said that because now I had a last name for him.

"What type of business does he have? I mean isn't he in jail for life for killing my mother amongst other things."

"Look, we can talk about this later, this isn't a good time."

He paused for a minute, "Ok...I love you Sasha...I really love you ok."

"Alright." I hung up.

I loved him too, but I just couldn't form the words to say it. I placed the phone in my purse. Jay was concerned.

"Ms. Jones, is everything Ok?"

"Everything is fine...And please call me Sasha."

He was back at ease and we continued our lunch. When we were finally at the hotel he walked me to my room. I couldn't stop smiling. During lunch I found out that Jay and I had a few things in common.

Back at my hotel door…

"Would you like to come in?" I asked innocently.

He smiled slyly. "Yeah, I think I can stay a minute, or two." I sat down at the little table and he sat on the couch.

I watched as he lifted his pants when he sat, I couldn't help but notice how big his imprint was. It was thick like a sausage roll and hung low to his thigh. My mouth began to water as thoughts about how delicious he was entered my mind. My thoughts were interrupted when I felt him gazing at me.

"Sasha, are you Ok?"

I broke my stare and looked down in embarrassment.

"Oh God I'm sorry...something just crossed my mind. I didn't realize I was in that deep of thought, it's kind of a habit, you know with me being a therapist...I always have to do a lot of thinking...sorry."

Jay shook his head like he understood but his eyes said different. He knew exactly what I was thinking about.

"Jay, do you know how long a life sentence is in the State of Delaware?"

He crossed his legs and sat back.

"35 years...I believe... Why are you ready to commit a crime?" he joked.

I giggled slightly, "No...but someone that is dear to me was sentenced to life in prison for murder. I just needed to know if life was until death."

His tone changed. He became more serious. "No...But if you don't mind me asking who is it?"

I sighed deeply. I didn't know how I was going to explain this without it sounding to off. But that was the issue. My situation was weird.

"It's my biological father. His name is Mixxon Diaz. I never knew him; he went to jail a year after I was born. It's just that I am getting ready to have a baby and I grew up without knowing my family. I want to give my child a chance at a real family. He's the only blood relative I have besides this baby that I know of." I rubbed my stomach.

He shook his head slowly.

"Do you know if it was a mandatory sentence or if he would be eligible for an early parole?" I shook my head in defeat.

"I know nothing, nothing at all about him. I just recently found out his name."

Just thinking about it made my eyes burn. All of this time my father was just moments away and I never knew it. Jay must have felt my sorrowfulness. He came over and gave me a, well at least it started as a friendly hug, but as time went on I don't think he wanted to let go.

He whispered, "Sasha, I am here if you need me. I will help

you as much as you want me to. Remember you are not alone."

I broke the embrace. I looked deep into his eyes, and I could see he was sincere and it scared me. Lorenz had made me feel the same way in the beginning and he betrayed me. Even if he is the real deal; I am married and a very pregnant woman. Plus he looked as if he were like 25 or 26 years old. But there was something familiar and comforting about him.

"Thanks Jay. Thank you very much. But don't you need to be enjoying yourself? You're still young you don't need to look over me."

He laughed. "*Young*...I am 33 years old."

I was astonished. He looked so young, and was so hip. "You're older than me. I'm 31."

"Yeah, I know." He walked to the door. "I got to run. I'll call and check on you tomorrow. Also don't forget what I said." And he was gone.

***

Camille

That sneaky bitch! How dare she lie to my damn face! That bitch was married to my Renzo, and he thought she was carrying his child. Oh she had some shit with her. I flicked through the channels trying to find my favorite soap opera. I gave up. This Direct TV shit was a headache. They had a million channels of bullshit that I didn't want to see. Whatever happened to the basic 3, 6, and 10? This shit had ABC1, ABC2, HBO 4, I threw the remote out of anger. Who needed fucking *'All My Children'* anyway?

I was living in my own soap opera since the day Lorenz found out Sasha was gone; his world was disrupted. He refused to work or eat, I was lucky he would at least shower. All he would do is wonder around the house; crying like a little bitch asking why did she leave! How did she find out! I want my wife; I need to be with my family!

I wanted to vomit.

He was even worse than Greggy. I was fed up. I called Miss Sasha, she didn't answer. I left her a message. The next day she calls sounding all giddy like she had no cares in the world. I let her know that I knew what she was up to and she better fix this shit, before I fixed her. I think she got the picture. No sooner than I hung up, he was running down the steps with his cell phone, to let me know it was her. I acted as if I cared.

Fuck that fat whore was my real thoughts.

I ventured out to my deck and enjoyed an apple martini. Spring was definitely here. The smell of fresh cut grass, the flowers were at bloom, and butterflies were fluttering. It gave me a slight sense of peace as I soaked in the scenery. I decided to call Shelly to see what was up with her. I hadn't talked to her for a minute.

"Hey Shellz, wassup Babe*?"*

"Hey Mee-Mee!" She sounded as if she had a few too many Martini's herself. "What ya doin?"

"What am I doing...the question is what are you doing?"

She got sexy on me. "I could be doin you," she giggled. That didn't sound too bad; my sex life had been zero since Renzo was losing his damn mind over his wife. I hadn't had a chance to get at that dick again.

"Why...you tryin to come see me..." I asked.

"Sure, why not. I can catch a flight tomorrow. Come get me from Philly. Oh yeah, is Lorenz down to play yet?"

"Girl...Lorenz is losing his mind over that whore Sasha! You know he married her right!"

I heard a loud scream come through the phone, "Shut the fuck up! He did what!"

She was so dramatic. I rolled my eyes. "Yeah girl, he married her and she packed up and left the day of the funeral. You know I think her and Greggy really had something going on."

"Girl, I may just drive down, he really needs us. I know together we can make him forget all about that bitch! I'll see ya in the morning." She hung up.

I hung the phone up satisfied. I knew that Shellz would do the trick. He couldn't resist her, and neither could I.

Later that day…

I was having my morning coffee when Shelly pulled up in her convertible Jaguar. She had quite a few suitcases with her, too many as far as I was concerned. I called to my housekeeper to help her with the luggage.

"Hey Shelly!" I gave her a big hug. It had only been a week since the funeral; I acted as if I hadn't seen her in years. "Girl look at you. I missed you so much."

She winked.

"Ditto…I am staying here as long as it takes to get our *Renzo* back to himself. After a few weeks with us, he'll be ready to sign divorce papers and forget all about Miss Sasha."

A few weeks?

"What about your job…You know the market is up...won't you be losing money?"

She smirked. "Money...What I need to worry about money for...Remember I was at the will reading baby, I know you got me...and besides, I can work from the office here...right...? You are cool with that."

I felt as if she was a little too sure of herself. But I agreed that she could work from the house. I reminded myself after our mission was accomplished, that I needed to check that bitch...She was a little too friendly with my money. I mean we were cool and all, but Lorenz and the money were mine. I helped her put her things away while I filled her in on the latest. We managed to stay out of his way most of the day. I wanted to surprise him with Shelly.

Later that afternoon, we went to the basement to play a game of pool. He was sitting at the bar and looked a little down. I didn't expect to see him in that type of mood. I mean just yesterday you would have thought he hit the lotto after he talked to Sasha. I walked over to him.

"Hey babe, everything Ok?"

I rubbed his shoulder. Shelly went behind the bar to make drinks.

"What's up Lorenz...You don't look to good."

She made him a Long Island Iced Tea, his favorite.

"Hey Shelly; I'm cool."

I sat next to him on the stool. "No you're not baby, what's wrong? I don't like to see you this way. I just lost your father and now it's like I'm losing you too. You haven't been feeling so great what's wrong?"

He took a deep breath. "I just got off the phone with Sasha and she was out to lunch with a man...she claimed he was a lawyer helping her with her dad's business affairs."

"Her dad?"

That through me for a loop.

What the hell was Miss Sasha up to?

He's in jail for killing your mom he had a life sentence, and business...The only business he had was dealing drugs."

He took a gulp of his drink. "I know...I just don't understand, it doesn't seem right. I still don't know how she figured all this out." I gave Shelly a look for help.

"Maybe Greg told her." she blurted. "I mean they were awfully close."

I looked at Shelly and secretly smiled. She was on point.

"You know she may be right. I mean didn't you say she had met him at the hotel the day of the accident. Maybe he told her then."

He shook his head.

"No I was there. He never had time to tell her."

"Did you ever find out why she was even going to see your father that late at night? She is *your* wife. Why was she meeting your dad at a hotel that late?"

"Now she is meeting this lawyer to help her father who killed your mother…what type of shit is that?"

Shelly is bad. She was really laying it on thick. From the look on his face our plan was working. "Do you even know where she is?"

He ran his fingers through his naturally wavy hair. I didn't know he had such nice hair until here recently. He was definitely in need of a haircut.

"No...I don't know. She said she can't tell me yet."

I sucked my teeth and acted as if I was utterly disgusted.

"She can't tell you...What the fuck! She's your damn wife...*and* she's pregnant."

Shelly's eyes bugged. I didn't tell her about the baby. Shelly took a shot of Jack to the head. She motioned for me to follow her to the pool table. I grabbed the bottle of Jack and followed. Lorenz was in deep thought. Our goal was accomplished, he was thinking hard about Miss Sasha and what she really was up to.

Shelly and I started playing. After a few games he joined us. We decided that the loser of each game had to take double shots of Jack, needless to say after a few hours we were all toasted. I went over to the flat screen and turned on a flick. I laid out on the floor, the room was spinning. I was really fucked up. Shelly joined me on the rug. He took a seat behind us on the couch. He kept looking at his cell.

"Are you expecting a call?" I teased.

"No. No not anymore." He placed the phone on the table and watched the flick. He was hurt, but I couldn't allow myself to feel sorry for him, I was on a mission.

I felt something tugging at my jeans. It was Shelly, she was about to start the show. I helped her slide them off. She started kissing my thighs, and nibbling near my clit. I pulled her shirt from over her head to expose her nice round melons. I caressed them and pinched at them as she sucked on my clit. I started to moan as her tongue traveled deep inside me.

I pulled her head to my face and kissed her passionately. Out the corner of my eye I could see he was bothered. He looked as if he wanted to leave, but something was keeping him there. I turned up the heat. I slipped my fingers into Shelly's dripping wet pussy and finger fucked her. I slurped up all her pussy juices while I was deep inside her with all four of my fingers. When Shelly was good and wet, I stuck my whole fist inside her. She began to gyrate her hips at a fast pace. I continued fucking her with my fist. She was moaning heavily in ecstasy as she reached her climax. I looked over for him, but he was gone. That's when I felt my head being pushed down into Shelly's pussy and his thickness being rammed in my pussy.

I laughed secretly within. Mission one…accomplished.

Chapter 23

Sasha

I expected to hear from Lorenz. I was surprised that it was now Tuesday and still no calls. I guess he was a little peeved when he heard Jay's voice. My little white lie I told about handling my father's affairs didn't help. I mean what was I to do? Jay was cool but I didn't want him to know who I was talking to.

I was finally in my new apartment. Jay and a few of his Frat brothers set up my bedroom furniture which arrived today. It was good seeing something familiar again. I decided I would buy all new furniture once the house was ready. I was relieved that the moving company agreed to pick up my belongings from the storage and bring them here. I gave them a healthy tip and treated them to lunch before they headed back up the road.

I couldn't believe that I could fit just about everything in that apartment that was once in my house. I went to the living room area and began to unpack my boxes that were marked pictures. The first one I grabbed was of Lorenz and me at the Disney Christmas parade. I held it next to my chest and closed my eyes. I wish I could have gone back to that moment. We were so happy. Things were starting to get better for us. Then New Years Eve flashed in my mind; Shelly sucking all over my husband and him standing there helpless. I put the picture back in the box and propped my legs up. They were still swollen. I had an appointment the next day to see my new doctor. I hoped she could give me an idea of what was going on with this. My face even seemed to be a little puffy. While I was lying there Jay walked in to see if I needed anything before they left. I told him I was fine and I would call him later. He rubbed my hand and told me to take it easy. I thanked them and they went their way.

***

My doctor was a Caucasian woman in her mid 40's. I told her about the swelling and how I had been extra tired, and had headaches. She told me that I had been passing protein in my urine and my blood pressure was high.

"Sweetheart, I believe you are developing pre-eclampsia. It can lead to toxemia if you don't be careful. You're going to have to be on bed rest for the remainder of your pregnancy. If your symptoms get worse, you'll have to be admitted in the hospital, until we deliver the baby. So, do you have anyone to help you at home?"

"Umm, I can get some help if needed."

She smiled, "Good. If you told me no I would have sent you to Wake Medical today. Go home and rest. I want to see you every week until the baby is born. You are at high risk. Ok sweetie, take care."

Damn, I was going to have to let Lorenz come here sooner than I thought. When I got home, I called him on my home phone to tell him the news.

He answered, "Yeah..."

I looked at the phone. He had a nasty tone.

"Yeah? Is that how you answer the phone Mr. Hayward?" I joked.

"So...I guess you're not on your date...So now you have time to call your husband?"

"Lorenz, what's wrong? I told you that he was an atto-"

"I know what you said Sasha. Oh...I see you're in North Carolina." He must have looked at the caller ID.

"Yes this is my house number. You can call me now. My cell bill is outrageous. I miss you."

"Oh you miss me now. You weren't missing me when you were out on your date with the attorney," he hissed.

Now I was getting irritated.

"Come on sweetie...I didn't call you to argue. I want you to come see me. I need you and I want to see my husband."

There was a long pause before he spoke again. "Sasha were you fucking Greg?"

I fell silent. I think my heart stopped. "What?"

"I didn't stutter Sasha. Were you fucking my dad? Is that baby mine or his?"

Where the hell did this come from?

I wasn't expecting to have to answer these questions so soon.

"Lorenz...Baby...Yes I did sleep with Greg. I thought you knew about it the first few times."

"THE FIRST FEW TIMES...SO IT WAS AN ONGOING THING? IS THAT EVEN MY FUCKING BABY!" He began to cry.

"SASHA, IS THAT MY BABY?"

The room felt like it was spinning out of control. "I DON'T KNOW...I DON'T FUCKING KNOW! I didn't mean to... I tried to stop but he wouldn't let me. I love you Lorenz, I really love you. Please believe me I didn't want it to come out this way. Greg got me pregnant on purpose he thought I was Rachael. You know he was crazy! This is *our* baby it doesn't matter who the father is. She's still apart of you."

I was so out of control that I let anything run from my lips.

"Camille was right about you! You are like your whore Mother!" And he hung up the phone.

I held the phone crying. What was I going to do? I couldn't do this alone. I waited for the dial tone and dialed a number.

"Hello..."

"Jay, its Sasha...I...I need you..."

***

Camille

I guess one would call it euphoria. That's how it's been around these parts. Lorenz was feeling much better now after a dose of Shelly and I. Days have passed and he hasn't picked up the phone once nor did he mention Sasha's name. My nights have been filled with complete satisfaction mostly from Shelly. I would get an occasional fuck from him.

The real estate market was booming. I was selling houses left and right. I had a convention coming up in Dallas that I had to attend. I think I had things pretty much together here and I didn't want him to have a Sasha relapse while I was gone.

Shelly and I were on the deck talking, discussing a shopping trip we were taking that weekend. We were interrupted by shouting in the sun room. We both went to investigate. It was Lorenz; he was crying and yelling on the phone.

Shelly whispered, “It must be Sasha.” I agreed.

We were both bent behind the door listening to every bit.

“Oh my God!” I whispered. She told him the truth. Shelly clapped her hands silently. I don't know if I was too happy about that. I didn't want her to tell him about our talk in the bathroom. I didn't want him to turn on me. He slammed the phone down and was headed in our direction. We both hurried to the kitchen and acted like we were about to make dinner. He punched the wall and I jumped.

He put a hole in my wall.

I was about to curse him out, but I didn't need my face to look like the wall. Shellz was the brave one. She grabbed him by the arm.

“Lorenz, this is not the answer. Baby you need to calm down. It's not worth it.” She hugged his neck tightly, “It's ok baby...You can cry, let it out. I know you're hurting.”

I felt jealousy set in.

What the fuck was she trying to do? I should be the one doing the consoling, this was my show, and she was over stepping again.

I walked over and grabbed him by the waist. I started to kiss him down his back. He grabbed my hands and pushed me away.

“Camille, not now...I can't do this shit now!” He walked away from both of us.

When he were out of hearing range Shelly started on me.

"Jesus Christ Me-Me, you just fucked it up."

"What!" I was disturbed.

"I fucked it up...What were you doing over there...Baby it will be alright...It's ok to cry...What are you, his fucking mother now?"

Shelly gave me the finger and walked away. *Stupid Bitch*! I wish I never let her in on the mission. Shit, after tonight I don't think I would need her anyway. Miss Sasha done told him everything now. Divorce papers will be in the mail soon. I fixed myself a Cosmo to celebrate.

After a few drinks I grabbed a bottle of Henny and two shot glasses to make up with Shelly. She made me sick, but I couldn't resist that big bodacious ass of hers, and that phat pussy. I almost tripped up the steps, I giggled. I was really fucked up, because it took me a minute to catch on to what I was seeing. All I saw was Shelly's ass jiggling as she bounced away on his dick. He was holding her waist lifting her up and down on his beam. Her body shuddered every time his balls slapped up against her ass. I watched them go at it; they didn't even notice I was there. I turned around and made my way to my room. I let Shelly have fun, because her ass was on her way out of here.

The next few weeks passed and still no word from Sasha. We all had a ball. Lorenz would come home from work; we all ate together, fucked together, and slept all in the same bed like one big happy family. However, I did notice that he didn't fuck me as much as he did Shelly. I mean he was really into it with her, like they were trying to make a baby or something. I couldn't complain, because he still showed me attention.

I almost hated to go away. The night before I left, he came in and gave me a private session. He did something that was odd. He pulled a condom out and put it on. I didn't say anything about it. God knows I didn't want any babies. I tried to kiss him, but he turned away. He just slid his dick in me and began to handle his business. I mean literally, business. No emotions. He just stabbed at my pussy, like he was trying to kill it. It felt awesome! He put my ass to sleep.

In the morning no one woke up to see me off. I guess

everyone was tired from the night before. I went to tell Shelly goodbye before I left and noticed she wasn't in her room. I walked a little further to his room and found them both in the bed hugged up. When I get back, her ass is leaving.

Chapter 24

Sasha

It seemed as if it took Jay two seconds to get to my apartment. I had left the door unlocked for him. I was lying in my bed holding my stomach crying. He climbed in the bed behind me and wrapped his arms around me. He didn't say a word, he just held me until I fell asleep.

When my eyes opened it was morning. I panicked when I noticed Jay next to me in the bed. *Not again*…I thought. I was relieved when I pulled back the covers and noticed that we were both fully dressed. I should have known better. He had been a perfect gentleman towards me since day one. He slept so peacefully reminding me of an angel; my guardian angel. I felt bad for hiding the truth about Lorenz and me from him. I had to tell him. He would find out sooner than later, but I would rather for him to find out from me, than anyone else.

I went to the bathroom to shower and change into more comfortable clothing. A pair of cotton capri's and a maternity shirt was today's fashion for me. I would get so mad when I visited the mall. Mimi Maternity had chic updated clothes; that is if you were a size 4 while you were pregnant. I had to opt for Dillard's or Motherhood, which made me look like a pregnant country mom.

I went into the living room and noticed Jay standing in the kitchen looking through the fridge. A typical man. I laughed to myself.

"Good morning sleepy head, whatcha looking for in there?"

He shut the door and flashed me a smile that could brighten Seattle. "Morning beautiful, how are you feeling?" He shut the door and made his way over to me. He sat alongside me and reached for my hand. "Are you ready to tell me what had you so upset last night?"

I forgot that we never had the chance to talk. I was an emotional wreck last night. I know he had to think I was halfway crazy the way I carried on. I instantly became embarrassed as I recalled my behavior.

"Jay I just don't know where to begin. It's so much to tell." He squeezed my hand.

"How about at the beginning?"

Again, I felt like one of my patients, unable to look him in the eyes, fearing what I may see. I said a short prayer for forgiveness, before I confessed my sins to this man who was not God and unlike him would most likely pass judgment on me.

About two hours and many tears later, Jay was aware of everything that occurred in my life within the last year. We both sat in silence staring straight ahead. I finally got up enough nerve to look his way. I studied his face, and it was blank. I didn't know if that was a good thing or not. Moments later, he got up from my side and headed back to the kitchen area

"You hungry?"

"Yes, just a little." *Was that it? Is that all he had to say after I spilled my innermost secrets to him.*

He looked inside the refrigerator, "You can't have any of this bacon, so how about some cheese eggs, grits, and bagels?" He began taking food out of the fridge to cook.

"Sure...But...Ummm...Did you pay attention to anything I just said?" I was a little bugged by his response or lack thereof. He pulled the pans from under the counter and began to prepare the food.

"Sasha if you are looking for me to judge you, that's not my job, only God can judge you. I had a feeling something wasn't too right anyway. I would have never thought you were married to his son. Dr. Hayward really had a problem, as well as your

husband. I'm just sorry you had to answer for your mother's wrong doing. And Camille, she never ceases to amaze me."
I held my head down in shame.

"Now, I can't tell you what to do about your marriage Sasha, but you need to rest and take care of yourself and that baby. All that other mess doesn't matter anymore. If Lorenz Jr. can't forgive you then that's on him. But from what I am hearing he needs to ask for your forgiveness. He pulled you into this Sasha, him and Dr. Hayward started this. You are the victim, stop beating yourself up."

He walked over and handed me my plate, "Eat this, and make sure you take your vitamin. I am going home to get ready for work. I'll send lunch over for you, and I'll be over tonight to fix your dinner."

I took the plate from him. Everything looked delicious especially the eggs they were fluffed like yellow clouds.

"Thanks Jay, but you don't have to do all this."

He kissed me on the cheek.

"I know I don't, but it's about time someone showed you what a true friend is."

Three weeks had gone passed and I still hadn't heard from my husband. Today was Good Friday and Jay was coming to take me out. I was happy because I hadn't been out at all; only to the doctor and sitting on my balcony for fresh air. He bought me this cute bronze and turquoise maternity dress to wear out. He picked me up around 7p.m. When we got in his car I asked him where we were going. He had on slacks, a shirt, and a tie. He was smiling.

"You'll see, there's someone I want to introduce you to."

I didn't ask any more questions. I sat back and enjoyed the ride. A few minutes later we pulled into a big white building that sat alone high on a hill. I had mixed feelings when I read the sign leading up to it. The Upper Room C.O.G.I.C.

"Church of God in Christ."

"Is there something wrong with that?"

I wanted to be like hell yeah there's something wrong. I loved God and everything. I sure wasn't ready to go up in a church, especially one in the country. I knew how church folk loved to be all up in other people's business.

"Oh...No...I just didn't expect to be going to church. I haven't been in years." I lied. I began to feel feverish all of a sudden. I broke out in a sweat.

Jay parked the car and walked over to my side of the car and opened the door for me.

"Are you Ok Sasha?"

"Yes, I'm fine. I think…" I took a deep breath, "I have so much hell up in me paranoia set in. Coming here got my demons in an uproar." I joked.

He held my hands, "You'll be alright, you're safe with me, but I don't know if your demons are?

We shared a laugh and walked into the church. It was packed for a Friday night. He greeted everyone as we passed through the vestibule. A few people smiled at us and gave hugs, while others huddled in corners looking in our direction with smug looks on their faces shaking their heads.

I knew this was a mistake I thought to myself.

Jay didn't seem the least bit affected by the stares. He continued to be polite and smile at everyone. An usher opened the doors to the sanctuary and led us down the aisle. I tried to sit in the back row but Jay didn't allow it. He tugged my arm and I followed behind him. The usher showed us to a seat on the first row next to this woman who was dressed to the 'T' with a big ol' canary yellow sequined hat that had to cost a fortune. With a matching two piece suit with yellow gloves. I couldn't help but notice the bling dangling from her wrist and ears.

This must be the Pastors' wife.

Jay leaned over and gave her a hug and whispered something to her. She smiled warmly and began to sing '*A Wonderful Change*' with the choir.

I must say that I enjoyed the service. He preached on the crucifixion. Listening to his sermon made me realize what I was going through wasn't that bad after all. I shed a few tears and even went up for prayer. They poured like a bottle of oil on my head. I never experienced that before. But I have to admit, I did feel better afterwards.

After church, Jay introduced me to the lady in the hat. She turned out to be Jay's mom… First Lady Duncan. His father was the Pastor of the church. She embraced me with so much love and invited me to dinner after church Sunday. I accepted her invitation. I guess I could come back to church, it wasn't that bad after all.

Chapter 25

Sasha

I can't believe it was May already. Only a few weeks left until I have my little one. It was Wednesday morning and I was waiting for Jay to come pick me up for my doctor's appointment. My health hadn't gotten any better. As a matter of fact, the swelling had become worse.

I had just hung up from Jay's mother. After she invited me to her home for Easter; we had developed a bond. She is a sweetheart. The whole family is wonderful; they treated me as if they've known me forever. Turns out that Jay is her only child, and she treats him like a baby. She calls me two and three times a day to check on me. She knows my situation, about me being married, and she prays for me about it. She believes that if it's God's will, we will be back together. That's also what I like about her, she is a devout Christian, but she doesn't try to push Scripture down my throat. She is there if I need to talk.

Jay came through the door with a huge grin on his face, dressed in one of his many designer business suits. Today he wore a navy blue suit with a sea green and navy paisley shirt underneath, with a short fat navy silk tie. He was very daring with his fashion style. But it worked in his favor.

"What has you all giddy?" I asked him. I didn't notice that he was on his cell.

"Oh my bad," I whispered.

He grabbed my phone and it began to ring. As soon as it

rang he hung up his cell.

"It's for you," he said smiling.

I hesitated and a funny feeling came over me.

"Answer it Sasha," he urged still smiling.

I slowly picked up the phone. "Hello."

"Sasha…."

There was a man on the other line with a raspy voice. Immediately a warm calming feeling came over me. I had no idea who this man was on the other line.

"Yes...Who am I speaking with?"

"Sasha...It's me your daddy...Mix..."

I dropped the phone. A lump that felt as huge as a softball formed in my throat. I didn't know what to do... I heard him saying,

"Hello...Hello...Sasha..." I put the phone back to my ear.

"Mixxon...Is this really my father?" I began to sob softly.

"Yeah baby girl, it's me. I thought I would never be able to talk to you. I thought we would never..." He started to get choked up. "I am so...so...sorry I wasn't there for you...and Rache...You and your sisters are my life."

"Sisters...I have Sisters?"

"Yes baby, you have one that's just a few months older than you. Her name is Jehaida, and Xiomara is a year older...You have nephews and nieces...My sister Rosa wants to see you so bad, she wants to bring your older sisters to see you. We thought we would never see you again."

I was lost for words. I held the phone crying. I finally managed to say, "I'm having a baby...and I want you to know how sorry I am about Greg...I didn't mean to."

"Baby...Greg wrote me and told me what he had done. We were at peace with each other before he died...He has to answer for what he did the same way I had to."

I was baffled. "He wrote you a letter...And that's all, he never sent you nothing else?"

"No, he sent me a letter in January. He told me how you looked so much like Rachael and he was drunk when he...you know…what he did to you. He was a sick man, Baby Girl. He was still in love with a dead woman who never loved him."

I was blown away. There were never any videos, that fucking Bitch Camille!

"Baby Girl, my time is up. Is it Ok if I give your information to your sisters and Rosa?"

"Sure Daddy...That's not a problem."

"We will talk soon. My time is up." The phone went dead.

I stood up and hugged Jay. "Thank you, thank you so much. You don't know what you just did for me...She lied I can't believe she lied about the video tapes."

Jay had snickered. Sweetie, inmates can't receive things like videos, didn't you know that?" I shook my head and buried my face in his chest. We held each other for what seemed to be eternity, until I felt something gush down my legs...Followed by severe pain...

***

Camille*....*

Yes! I am finally home. Those bastards blew me off the whole entire time I was in Dallas. Every time I called, Shellz would rush me off the phone. When I called Renzo's cell he would either be too busy to talk or Shelly would answer it. They were getting a little too close for comfort.

"Shelly...Lorenz..." I called for them. "Is anyone home? Shellz...You here honey?" Elsa, my housekeeper came from the kitchen.

"Mrs. Hayward, Mr. Lorenz and Ms. Shelly went out for dinner. Can I help you with your bags?"

"No, Sweetie. I'm ok. Elsa, you can have the night off ok." She thanked me and went to gather her things.

Dinner...He never takes me out to dinner. I carried my things to my room. I undressed and slipped into my lounging clothes. I went to the bar, and grabbed my Jack. I had to get right, because I had a lot to get off my chest when they got back.

Four hours later, he and Shelly showed up. They were laughing and joking. Shelly was hanging all over his arm. He was glowing. That made me really angry. I wouldn't have minded if it were me who made his radiance appear. I hadn't seen him look like that since Sasha was here. They were about to walk right pass me when I cleared my throat loud enough so they would notice me. The giggling ceased.

"Oh, hey Camille." She said blandly. "When did you get back?" She walked over and dropped in the chair in front of me. She was wasted.

I rolled my eyes at her and turned my attention to him.
He ignored my presence and began stroking her weave and planting little pet kisses on her forehead.

"Be careful honey. You better hope it doesn't come out." I was being sarcastic.

They continued showing each other affection. My stomach began to churn.

"So Camille how was your conference?" He finally asked.

"Baby, it was so, so, boring." I jumped up and ran over to him like a lost puppy who finally found its master. I ran my fingers down his back.

"I missed you so much. I was so lonely." I continued to lay it on thick.

"You know I just feel so empty without my Greggy. But you, you fill that void for me." I slipped my hands around his waist and buried my head in his back.

Out of know where. They both burst out into loud laughter. He removed my hands from around his waist. I was hurt and confused. Shelly was doubled over in laughter. She was taking shit too far. It wasn't that funny.

"What is so funny? I am in mourning over my husband...I am hurt, and you think it's funny?" I was livid. So livid that out of nowhere I slapped the hell out of her.

She stopped laughing immediately.

She stood up quickly like she was about to attack me. Lorenz grabbed her.

"No, Lorenz let me go." She attempted to break away from him. He was too strong she couldn't budge.

"Go ahead let that Bitch go!" I took my earrings off and

kicked off my shoes. I was tired of her fake ass, and it was time for me to put her in her place.

"That's ok I got your bitch. I bet Lorenz didn't know the only reason why you want to be with him is to get his father's money. I bet you didn't tell him that!" she laughed devilishly. Lorenz had a confused look on his face.

"Oh she didn't tell you about all the money that your daddy left for his first born grandchild?"

I couldn't believe she went there. I really wanted to knock that bitch's head off. But I would have the last laugh.

"First of all Koshell, you need to get your shit right. There is no trust fund for his first born, because she signed it away!"

"Who signed what away? How would Sasha know anything about the trust if she left the morning of the funeral? She wasn't here for the reading...." His nostrils were flaring he was furious.

I fell silent. I just messed up.

"I don't know what she's talking about." I lied.

Shelly began to laugh. "Yeah right...You made her sign them in the bathroom."

"Shut the fuck up, you stupid cunt!" I was infuriated. I know damn well this bitch wasn't turning her back on me.

"He already knows. I told him everything Camille. I told him how you wanted to marry him, so you could get the trust fund, if Sasha's baby turns out not to be Greg's then that money is forfeited and goes to him." She put her finger in my face.

"I also know how you set up a fake reading for me so I could go along with your plan to get Lorenz away from Sasha. It's all out MeMe. It's ova for you."

"You know she's lying right? I know how much Sasha meant to you...I wouldn't do that." The look on his face was demonic. I never saw anything like it, and I was frightened.

He started to come towards me with fire in his eyes and his nose flaring. I began to back up in fear.

"What do you have to say for yourself Camille?"

"I did it for you. She wasn't any good for you. She had to go. For God sake Lorenz she was sleeping with your father!"

We were now face to face. Nothing between us but the air we

breathed.

"So you were just looking out for me? Is that it?"

His voice softened although it was still filled with authority.

"Yes Lorenz...we are family and she was going to tear us apart just like her mother did. Rachael made your father go mad. I couldn't let that happen to you."

I embraced him and he just stood there.

For a moment, I thought everything was all good. Then he grabbed me by neck tightly with one hand. His grip was strong and he was scaring me. I struggled to get away.

"What are you doing? Get off me Lorenz! You're hurting me!"

He threw me to the couch and struck me several times across my face before Shelly pulled him away.

"That's enough! Lorenz please stop you're going to kill her!" she begged him.

Blood was pouring from my mouth and nose. Our eyes connected and hurt and anger engulfed him. Without saying a word he went towards the steps with Shelly in tow.

I was devastated. I couldn't believe that he went off on me like that. I thanked God that Shelly was there who knows what would have happened if she didn't stop him.

Chapter 26

Camille

In my line of work you meet a lot of people. If you treat them right, there's nothing they wouldn't do for you. Dr. Cho was one of those people. A few years ago I sold him and his wife their house at an amazing price. They were very grateful and vowed that anytime I needed them to call and they would be there. I never took him up on his offer until now.

After my life shattering experience with Lorenz. I knew I needed medical assistance. I didn't want to call the ambulance, which meant the police would come. I didn't want anyone to be arrested. I damn sure wasn't going to go to the hospital on my own so they could ask a million questions. I remembered little ol' Dr. Cho and decided to call him. So he came over and examined me, gave me a few stitches, a bottle of Vicodin and told me to take it easy.

I suffered with excruciating pain for days and no one even came to see about me. I tried to figure out a way to redeem myself. I refused to let Shelly win. There was no way I was letting her get Lorenz...If I couldn't have him. I would rather see him with Sasha. I needed a plan. I had to come up with something fast.

The next few weeks went by fast; Lorenz and Shelly continued being love birds. They were fucking all over the house. I walked in on them a few times. I just acted as if it didn't bother me. At night they were really ridiculous, I could hear Shelly screaming all the way down the hall. One night, I even thought I heard her scream she loved him, too. I turned over in my bed, yeah right. He loves that pussy. His heart was with Sasha.

"Me-Me...We got to go!" Shelly ran into my room panicking.

"What...What's wrong?" I thought something happened with Starla...

"It's Sasha...She's been rushed to the hospital...I was in the office when he left. There was a note on the table saying he was going to Duke University Hospital."

"Damn...I wonder what's up. That baby wasn't due until June..."

"Yeah, I know...I hope nothing happens to her...he will be devastated."

I had to catch myself from laughing. This bitch really thought she had him figured out.

"Let me throw something on, I can buy something while we're there."

I called in a favor from one of my high profile clients. He had access to a private jet. I refused to miss any of this.....

***

Sasha

"Oh my God...It hurts...It hurts so bad…."

Jay had called the ambulance as I had gone into labor. My water ruptured and it looked like they were going to have to give me an emergency C-section. I gave Jay my cell phone for him to call Lorenz. Everything was going so fast. They were hooking me up to all these machines. My blood pressure had shot up into well over the 200's so they were giving me magnesium. They were doing an ultra sound to see if the baby's head had turned downward.

Jay came in for support, "Did you speak to him?"

"Yes baby, he's on his way here now."

I didn't like the look Jay had on his face, he seemed a little agitated.

Dr. Saos came in and studied the baby's heart monitor.

"Is this the father?"

"No ma'am this is my good friend, the father is on his way."

"Ok…I see…well sir could you please excuse us while I discuss a few things with Mrs. Hayward."

Jay turned to leave but I grabbed his arm.

"NO, it's ok he needs to know what's going on with me, he's my support person, and he's in charge of any decisions that need to be made when I can't make them."

Jay looked at me real skeptical. I shook my head in reassurance.

She told us that since I was only 33 weeks, they weren't sure how the baby's lungs were. They wanted to try and hold off for a few days, but the sac is completely dried out so they are going to have to take the baby.

She grabbed my hands. "Sasha dear...Don't worry your baby will be just fine." She patted my hands, and told Jay to follow her so he could get prepared to go in the surgery room.

When we entered the surgical room, I immediately began to shiver.

"I'm so cold."

Dr. Saos said, "It's the medicine, you'll be ok...ok...Sasha honey we are getting ready to prepare for your daughter's birth."

She put a blue drape up so I couldn't see what was going on. I felt them wipe something on my stomach. Jay held my hand and squeezed. I think they started to cut, because I felt pressure and tugging.

"Are you ok?" Jay asked I nodded.

"Ok Sasha dear...We have cut through the layers of skin and we see your little girl's head..."

Jay went around the drape and began filming. The pressure became a little more intense.... Then I heard a gloppy noise followed by a loud cry.

"And here she is you mind if your friend here cuts the cord?"

I gave Jay the ok. Another doctor took the camera and filmed while Jay cut her cord. Then she plopped her right in front of me. She was BIG...and she had all this hair...She had a set of lungs on her.

"Look at your baby...She is beautiful." Jay was happy; I saw it in his eyes.

The nurses took the baby and did whatever they had to do over in the corner. Jay bent down and kissed me on the cheek.

"You did great...She's gonna be fine. You both are going to be fine..." was the last words I heard before drifting off to sleep.

Chapter 27

Sasha

I thought it was all a dream my conversation with my dad, and the baby being born. When I opened my eyes I expected to see Jay at my side, instead it was Lorenz staring at me. He looked empty. He seemed to be in deep thought. He didn't even notice that I had opened my eyes.

"Lorenz…." My voice was faint, "Did you see her?" He held my hand.

"Yes, she's beautiful. She looks just like you...she looks just like your family."

I didn't know what he was insinuating. I wasn't in shape to argue. So I just ignored his comment.

"Where is she? Where is Jay? What time is it?"

I looked around the room and noticed the clock. It was 10 a.m. I knew that wasn't possible, because I had her at 12:30 in the afternoon.

"Did something happen?"

Lorenz let go of my hand. "I don't know. Ask your *friend* to fill you in. I didn't get here until 7p.m. last night. They wouldn't let me in because your spokesperson didn't have me down on the list. I had to wait for another man to give me permission to see my wife and daughter."

He was trying his hardest to keep his composure. It wasn't working aversion had shown its face.

"I'm sorry. What else was I to do? You weren't here."

"And whose fault was that? Why didn't you tell me you were sick? Never mind, I don't know why I asked. You don't seem to want to tell me anything...."

Just as I was about to say something; Fric and Frac burst through the doors. Camille and Shelly strut in bearing gifts.
Camille didn't look like herself. She seemed to be a lot thinner and older looking.

"Hey Miss Sasha...that baby is gorgeous...But she doesn't look nothing like Lorenz. His genes are strong...I mean just look at Renzo and Greggy, they were a splitting image...." Camille pulled a chair up to my bed.

Shelly rolled her eyes. "Congratulations on the baby Sasha...She is cute. She has Renzo's eyes. But she looks more like your family."

"Thanks" I said flatly.

"Starla sends her love. She wanted to come, but she had other more important things to do."

I wanted to reach over and punch Camille in her face. I thought back to what my dad said. How he never received videos; she made it all up.

"So what are you going to name the baby?" That came from Shelly. I noticed she was standing next to Lorenz awfully close. When he moved she was on it like he was a magnet.

"Azariah Becca Hayward...." I looked at Lorenz for his approval. He put his head down.

"Aww, that's cute. She's naming her after your dead mother, that's so sweet."
Everyone turned their attention to Camille with a look of shock.

"Camille, you really have a sweet fucking way with words, that shit was wrong!" Shelly reprimanded. I watched both of their expressions toward each other. I sensed an attitude between the two. Something was definitely up. Camille huffed and rolled her eyes. She turned her attention back to me.

"Anyway, when will you two have a DNA test done? You can't keep us all in suspense for too long."

That was enough; I had it with this chick.

"Camille, mind your business. That's between my husband,

in case you forgot, and I to deal with." I stressed. I was ready to say more but was interrupted.

"I already took care of it…." Lorenz spoke. "I had the test done this morning. We will have the results in a few days."

I was shocked that he had the test done so quickly.

"I still say she looks nothing like your family...Lorenz, she's not even dark around the ears, and she looks like Miss Sasha's people."

"Camille...how do you even know what the hell my family looks like?" I said.

My door opened and Jay came in followed by two women.

"Hi Jay!" I said trying to sit up in the bed.

He put a vase full of fresh flowers on the table.

"I have someone who wants to meet you."

The older of the two woman walked up to me with tears in her eyes...She had long jet black hair that hung down to her waist. She had a mocha complexion. She was very pretty. She had to be in her early 40's. She rolled her R's when she spoke.

"Oh...My baby...You look just like Rachael, oh my God...I can't believe it's you Sasha...I'm your Aunt Rosa...Xiomara...come meet your sister Sasha!"

Xiomara walked over to me and hugged me. She had a short cut like I used to sport, and she had a honey brown complexion and hazel eyes.

"Oh my God...My sister...I heard so much about you...Finally."

We were all crying. I had forgotten all about my other company until Camille blurts out. "Well you can finally meet the family of the killer responsible for your mother's demise."

Everyone just stopped and stared at Camille. Lorenz stormed out and Shelly followed behind, but not before she slapped the shit out of Camille.

Camille glared at Jay while holding her face, and ran out the room embarrassed. We all tried to hold in the laughter, but it was too much, it came out. Rosa and Xiomara pulled up chairs next to my bed. Jay stood next to me stroking my hair.

"You know you scared us for a minute, you acted like you

didn't want to wake up." He said softly.

"What happened...And where is Azariah?"

"That's her name?" He asked. I nodded. "That's beautiful..."

My head was a little woozy. I smiled.

"Azariah, she is in the N.I.C.U, her blood sugar was a little low, and they want to keep an eye on her for a couple of days before she is moved up here with you."

"When can I see her?" I was anxious to see my baby.

"I checked with the doctor, she said maybe later this evening I can wheel you down if your pressure stays steady. They want you to stay calm and rest...By the look of things...I can see that's not happening."

He had a concerned look on his face. "So, did you like your surprise?" He smiled and looked at my aunt and sister.

"Thank you, Jay...How did you know how to get in touch with them?"

My Aunt Rosa answered, "Mixx called me yesterday morning. He told me he had spoken to you. And he gave me your number. I called and no one answered, so I left a message on your machine. Two hours later your friend here called me and told me about the baby, I was so excited he asked if I could get your sisters and come down. Xiomara lives around the corner, so I saw her outside and told her. She called Jehaida, but she couldn't get off work. So a member of your church picked us up yesterday afternoon and now we're here." Her accent was strong...You wouldn't have thought she was in the U.S. long.

"Thank you for coming...You don't know how much this means to me...That I actually have family."

Jay acted like he was offended. "So what am I? Chopped liver?" He laughed, "You always had a family; my parents adore you, and so does the Upper Room Members. You and Azariah are a part of us."

He caressed my thigh and stared gently in my eyes. We just gazed at each other with admiration for a moment. An uncomfortable look emerged on his face and he stood up.

"Well, I am going to get ready and get out of here. I will call you in a little bit; I need to talk to you about some business. Rosa and Xiomara, you can call Deacon Jones when you are ready to go back to the hotel." He kissed me on the forehead and Aunt Rosa and Xiomara on the cheek.

When Jay was out of site Xiomara leaned over and whispered in my ear.

"Girl, he likes you." She was cheesing all hard.

Aunt Rosa hit Xiomara in the arm. "Stop it...She is a married woman…but he does like you." She added with a smile.

Xiomara threw her hand in the air as to wave her off.

"Married...ha, ha I can't tell the way that chick with the blonde weave was all on him, you would have thought that was her man." She snarled her face up.

I shook my head in disgust. She was talking about Shelly. Her look went from Pocahontas to Beyonce; she had this overly sized blonde weave going on. She looked like Simba or better yet Mufasah from the Lion King. I began to laugh quietly to myself, but the pain stopped me. Rosa noticed the discomfort on my face.

"You alright Sweetie? You need me to get the nurse?" I nodded. Rosa left the room to get help. Xiomara held my hand and apologized.

"I wasn't trying to cause trouble, but your husband and that chick did seem like they were together and that bitch with an attitude that was with them was really jealous. They got some freaky shit going on. You betta watch that." She sat on the edge of my bed.

I listened to her words carefully. Something definitely was going on. I just wasn't too sure if I really wanted to know the details.

Chapter 28

Sasha

A few hours later I woke up again. I didn't even know I had fallen asleep. Xiomara was sitting next to me reading a magazine. I tried to move my head, but it was so heavy. I was really doped up. She must have heard my movement. She sat the magazine down and directed her attention to me.

"Hey sis...You need help with the pillow?"

I opened my mouth to speak but nothing came out. My throat and mouth was so dry from all the medications. She positioned the pillow for me and smiled.

"So, where is everyone?" My voice was croaked horribly.

"Well, Aunt Rosa is out with Mrs. Duncan. Your husband and those two chicks left a while ago. He said something about a graduation he had to get ready for, but he did stop in to see the baby before he left. He came in here for a moment, when he saw me he left back out with an attitude. I know he's pissed about what Papi did but damn that was so many years ago and I ain't do shit to him, so why treat me funny you know...." She talked so fast I barely caught what she was saying.

I did however hear what she said about Lorenz. I couldn't believe that he didn't wait for me to wake up before he left. I thought about what Xiomara said about him and Shelly. I wondered if they were together. Xiomara was staring me down waiting for me to answer her question.

"I'm sorry about the way he is acting; he is going through a lot right now. He just lost his father, and we aren't really doing that great. It's just a big mess."

She shook her head as to say she understood his issues. "I heard about G's death, it was all in the newspapers. Aunt Rosa wanted to go to the viewing but she heard they wasn't having one so we just sent flowers." That threw me for a loop completely.

"G? Are you talking about Greg? You knew Greg?"

"I don't know him personally, but everybody has heard of him. That shit is legend around our way...How Pops tried to shoot Greg and Becca jumped in the way. She was like a modern day Juliet. She took a bullet for her man. That was straight suicide. Then you marry his son, that's some straight soap opera shit!"

I laughed, she had a point. I could tell Xiomara was going to be a piece of work. She was so straight forward about everything. I was happy she was here. It's just hard to believe that I had family so close but yet so far.

She sat back in the chair and crossed her arms, "So...What you gonna do about Beyonce Jr.? She's trying to take ya hubby...If she ain't *already* got him."

I sighed, "I don't know...Xiomara...I really don't know." I sat back in the bed.

She sat silent for a moment and then changed the subject.

"Jehaida called, she said she'll be down this weekend," she sucked her teeth and shook her head side to side. "You know she's going to bring them bad ass kids with her."

I smiled.

"It can't be that bad. How many does she have?" She laughed out loud.

"Not, bad! Ok well how about she has five of them bastards, stair steps. The oldest is fifteen, and her ass is out of control...She fuckin and everything. The youngest is ten and he has ADHD, he's off the hook."

I laughed.

"So where is the husband?"

She laughed. "Ain't nobody marrying her with them crazy ass kids."

We both laughed.

"So, are you guys full Dominican?"

"No my mother is from Puerto Rico, Jehaida is like you...Her mom is black. You two look more alike. My two girl's father is black. He's in jail. You'll meet them next time we visit. They're a mess. Shay is six and Shavaun is nine." Her cell phone rang. "I'll be right back."

She left out the room. Fifteen minutes later, she came back in pushing an incubator. Behind her were Mrs. Duncan, Rosa, and a few of the women from the church.

"Surprise!" They all yelled.

They were giving me a baby shower. I was so surprised. She handed me the baby. She was bundled up in a pink blanket. Her face was practically covered with the blanket. I gently moved it down to get a good look at her face. Her face was so fat; she had the biggest cheeks and chinky eyes. I tried to get her to open her eyes, but she wouldn't budge. She reminded me of a black Gerber baby. I couldn't stop kissing her. I tuned out everyone around me; my focus was on her. She was my world. I took her little pink hat off, to check out her hair.

Thank God.

It looked like she was gonna have the good stuff like me. It was soft and jet black loose curls. I ran my hand through them. I examined her features closely, they were right; she didn't look much like the Hayward's at all. I pulled her little hands and feet out of the snug blanket to count fingers and toes. I had to make sure they were all there. They were. She was perfect.

"I love you...I love you so much." I whispered.

When the party was over, they took Azariah back down to her floor. Everyone was gone and I was just about to go to sleep. I heard the door open and noticed Jay creeping in.

"Hey Sasha, are you awake? If so can I talk to you for a minute?"

"Sure, what's up?"

"I have some good news. Your house is ready. I wanted to know if you wanted me to set the baby's things up in the nursery for you." He pulled a chair up next to me and held my hand.

"Wow...That's great, but I'm not quite ready to move in. I haven't bought any future for the house. I don't want to carry any of my old furniture over there. I want a fresh new start. I decided to stay at the apartment for a few more months. Do you mind setting up in the spare room at the apartment?"

"Sure. No problem. When do you want to look for furniture for the house? Wait...Let me stop I'm overstepping my boundaries...That's you and your husband's job." He held his head down.

I brushed my hand along his arm and reassured him. "Jay, baby you're my friend for life. You are not overstepping your boundaries. As a matter of fact...I was going to ask you to be Azariah's God father."

"I will be honored. Are you sure that's not going to be an issue with your husband?"

"It doesn't matter if it is...He's not even here you are."

Chapter 29

Camille

On the flight back home I didn't speak to Shelly. Her and Lorenz sat together all cuddled up. I could have sworn once he saw the baby and Sasha, his feelings would change. Boy was I fooled. He was even more disappointed. She looked nothing like his black ass. Then Sasha had the Diaz Dynasty there and I can't forget about that fine man she had catering to her.

He had his whole family in the lobby, like he was the damn daddy. He was hot, when he tried to see his wife and they asked if he was James Duncan. He cursed that poor nurse out! I snickered. The look on his face when he saw Rosa and Xiomara was priceless. Sasha was not shedding tears over his ass. She was living her life with her new found family. Lorenz was yesterday's news. Shelly...oh, I can't believe how she showed off in front of them people. Like she really cared. She acted as if she was the wife visiting the mistress. I know Sasha's sister peeped the whole thing. Shelly better back off. She knows them Spanish people like to slice folks up. She's from N.Y. so she should know better.

Starla was in the kitchen when I returned.

"Hey baby, she had a girl." She ignored me and continued to eat her food. I sat my purse on the table. "Starla darling, don't act like that. I had to go check on the new edition to our family."

She looked around me and watched him and Shelly head up the steps. She put her fork down.

"So, are you both sharing him now?" She followed me with her eyes around the kitchen.

I acted as if I didn't hear her.

"I know you heard me. Ok, let me speak your language. Are you and Shelly both fucking Renzo?" She said with a nasty tone.

I slammed the fridge door and pointed my finger at her. "Now you listen here Star. You don't talk like that to me. I'm your mother!" I tried to be firm.

She hopped off the stool, "You didn't answer my question. Are you and the flakey lesbo fucking my stepbrother?"

I went to slap her and she grabbed my hand. "If you put your hands on me, I'll have you arrested...I know what you do. I know I have a money hungry slut for a mom...Everyone knows!"

I couldn't believe what was going on. First Shelly, then Lorenz, and now my own daughter is turning on me."

"Starla, I'm your mother...How can you talk to me this way? You're hurting me...Can't you see that!" I cried. "I do everything for you...You have this nice house...You go to an exceptional school, you have everything! I lost my husband!"

She laughed insanely, "Your husband, you hated him! You were jealous, because he didn't love you the way he loved Sasha. I bet you didn't know that I knew they were having an affair. I know more than you think. Especially how you are, hell everyone knows how you are. You use people...You used Greg the same way you're using Lorenz...And that school...I'm not going back to that school! Everyone knows that you're a slut. They talk about me, Mommy. They talk about my slutty mom. And the boys, they think I'm just like you, BLACK SLUTTY...TRASH! I know everything! Everything! I even know the truth about my dad; I know that you blackmailed him."

I was confused. "Who told you that? That's not what happened. How do you know anything about him?"

"You threatened to tell his wife about me. That's why he gave you all that money. You told me my dad was dead, but he's not..." She cried, "My dad came to see me...in school... Why didn't you tell me the truth! I hate you...I hate you so much!"

I tried to hold her. "I'm so sorry Starla...baby. I was going to tell you the truth when you were older. I'm so sorry."

She cried in my arms...and said, "I also know that Greg's death wasn't an accident...I know that you did it Mommy."

Sasha

My baby was now four days old. She was finally released from the N.I.C.U. They brought her to the little nursery connected to my room so she could be with me. I was changing her diaper when my phone rang. I picked up the phone and told them to hold on before they could speak. I finished putting the diaper on and laid her in her bed.

"Hello..."

"Hey Sweetie, how's my little girl?" Lorenz said kindly.

"Oh, she's great. I just put her to sleep...Did you say *you*r little girl?"

"Yeah...I did. I got the results back today. Sasha, she's ours. She is our little girl." I could imagine the smile on his face.

I wonder how he got the results back so fast. It usually takes about six weeks to get results. I was excited.

"Are you serious? Why didn't they give me a copy of the report?"

"They will, I told them to fax it to your floor. Sasha...You don't know what this means to me...I want to apologize for being an asshole."

"I know, baby...We both made mistakes. Now we can put this behind us and we can start our family."

"I know. Now you can come back home with me...And things can be like they use to be..."

I was a little hesitant...I didn't want things how it used to be. I wanted to start over...

"I...I am home now...My home is here...I can't go back to West Chester...Too many bad memories...I can't go back to that place."

"We don't have to go there...I accepted a job here in Baltimore at John Hopkins. We can start over here." I forgot today was his graduation.

"Congratulations! How was the ceremony?"

"It was nice. Camille, Shelly, and Starla were here to support me." It seemed as if he was throwing their presence in my face.

"You know I would have been there if...I wasn't in the hospital recovering from the birth of your daughter." I said defensively. I hated the fact that she always seemed to be in the picture. I was so through with them...He must have noticed that I was becoming cynical. His voice lightened up.

"I am driving down in the morning to stay until you're released. I guess I will come down on the weekends until I have a home for us here and you a chance to get things in order for your move..."

I can see he was not going to respect my decision on staying here. I decided not to comment on his last statement. I was in no mood to argue, we could tackle that situation another time.

"Why can't you come down tonight?" I whined.

I had to admit these last few months Jay had been great to me. Yet, I still missed my husband.

"Baby, Shelly is throwing me a huge graduation party at the Hilton tonight. I can't leave after all she's done for me I owe it to her."

A deep feeling of rejection set in. My mind began to wonder.

What did she do for him that I didn't? I just laid here and had this man's baby, and he's putting us on hold for her. I just didn't get it.

"Ok Lorenz...I guess I'll see you tomorrow...I love you."

"Kiss my lil girl for me." He hung up.

I held the phone in front of my face in disbelief.

Did he not hear me say I love you? He didn't even have the decency to say it back. The more I thought about the conversation that just took place the more irritated I became. If our marriage had any hope we were going to have to be far away from Shelly and Camille. I decided I would tell him face to face, that I was not moving to Baltimore. Our home was in

North Carolina.

The next morning Jay and Xiomara came in with arms full of catalogs; Ethan Allen, Baby's R Us, Home Interior to name a few and others. We sat on the bed laughing and joking while picking out items for my new home. A few hours later Xiomara took a break; that gave me a chance to talk with Jay alone. I moved over on my bed and made room for Jay.

"I need to talk to you for a minute honey."
A serious look came on his face as he sat next to me. I told him about Lorenz coming down, and trying to get me to move to Baltimore.

"So Azariah is his?" He asked.

"Yeah." I reached in the drawer to show him the fax. He looked it over.

"It's legit...It says here he's 99.9% the father. So what do *you* want to do?" I could see the look of disappointment on his face.

"First of all...I want you to know nothing will change between us. You have been a great friend to me and you are an important part of my life, both of our lives. Jay, I don't know what I would have done without you." I felt tears falling. "Your family took me in, you made it possible for me to meet my sister and Aunt. You brought my dad into my life. You filled voids, you gave me hope, everything. You helped me change my life. I love you for that...I love you...I really love you."

My heart began to beat fast. Jay moved closer to my face. I could practically taste him we were so close. I looked into his eyes and he had the look of desire. He airily mouthed, "I love you too."

I had a feeling that the unimaginable was about to happen; something that I secretly longed for. I closed my eyes to wait for it, but he stopped.

"Um-Hmm" Xiomara interrupted, carrying Azariah in her arms. "Umm, I'm not trying to spoil the moment...But I wanted to warn you that your husband is on his way to the room."

I scooted away from Jay. Damn I had forgotten that he was coming today. That quick?

Jay stood up and cleared his throat. "So, these are the items you want? I'll place the order for you." He said nervously. "Do you want me to use the business account to purchase them, because you know most of it's a tax write off." He smiled.

"Sure...Use that." He patted my leg and left.

Xiomara shot me a sneaky grin and handed me my child.

"Naughty...Naughty." She shook her finger at me. Lorenz walked in. She rolled her eyes and smiled "Let me give you two sometime alone."

"No wait...I want to introduce you to my husband." She stopped and waited. Lorenz turned his nose up and looked her up and down, and kept coming towards me. Xiomara bunched up her face and gave him the finger behind his back. She exited the room.

Lorenz sat down and took the baby from my hands. I wasn't feeling him at all.

"That was real fucking ignorant...That's my sister!" I was agitated.

He tried to sound cordial, "Baby, you don't even know her. I damn sure don't need to know her ghetto ass!"

"What! Ghetto, don't talk that way about my family...I never said anything about your fucked up demented daddy."

He laughed sarcastically.

"He must not have been that fucked up, you were fucking him, and watch your mouth around my daughter...." He began to play with her fingers and cooing at her.

"So, where are you staying at these days?" He asked.

I couldn't believe how quickly his demeanor changed. First he was jumping down my throat then he was cool as a cucumber. *This man is Bi-Polar for sure,* I thought.

"I have an apartment."

"Wow, you went from a house to an apartment...Are you working? How are you maintaining your bills? I know your money ran out from your old job."

He was being smart again. So I decided to feed into his ignorance.

"Yeah that money is gone, but my "father" had things put up for me. He made sure that I would be taken care of."

That must have gotten under his skin because his expression changed once again. His nose flared and he began to take deep breaths.

I bet he thinks I'm referring to Mixxon. His dumb ass didn't even know I was talking about his daddy.

"So you're using dirty money to take care of yourself? That's positive."

I shot back, "All money is dirty honey; it all spends the same..." I was tired of the games. "Lorenz, you know I'm tired of this bickering back and forth. We have a child to think about...Are we going to work this out or what?"

Azariah began to cry and he handed her to me. He folded his hands together and sat back in his chair. I grabbed one of the pre-made bottles and began to feed her, while he watched.

Noises from Azariah slurping her milk was only heard for silence had grown between us. Moments later he stood up and walked towards the door. Before walking out he looked me in the eyes as if he was looking deep into my soul.

"We can try to make this work, but so much has changed. I'm not the same person Sasha...You're not the same...and *we* will never be the same."

I had no idea what he meant. I had a bad feeling that I was soon going to find out.

Chapter 30

Sasha

The baby and I had been home for two weeks. Things had been very hectic. Lorenz was gone yet again. He decided to commute between North Carolina and Baltimore. That way he could keep his job and spend time with his family. Things seemed to be getting better between us. We hadn't argued since that day in the hospital. Xiomara and Aunt Rosa went back home the day I was released. Lorenz made them feel very unwelcomed. I apologized for his behavior, but they didn't let his ill-mannered behavior keep them away. I spoke with them quite often.

Jay was still a big part of my life; he stopped by every other day even though the visits were quite brief. A few days ago, he took me by the house to see how it was coming along. It was now completely furnished. It was beautiful. He wanted to know if I was ready to move in. I told him I wanted to wait a little longer. I can tell he couldn't quite understand why I wanted to be crammed in an apartment, when I had this beautiful home. I had my reasons for it; I just wasn't ready to share them.

Earlier today, I was sterilizing bottles when my door bell rang. I opened it and it was Mrs. Duncan. I gave her a big hug and she came in. I asked her if she wanted any tea or coffee. She told me she would be here for just a minute. She needed to talk to me about something. I turned the pot off and sat on the couch next to her.

"Is everything Ok?" I asked.

"I was about to ask you the same question." She said.

"I'm fine, the baby is fine."

"Is there something going on between you and Jay?" I was dumbfounded.

"No...We are friends. I mean I do care about him...I'm married...Mrs. Duncan, and I'm trying to do things right since I gave my life to the Lord...."

She wasn't buying it. "Honey...I know you're married on paper, but what you have is not a marriage...There is so much chaos going on, I can see it...I love you Sasha. God knows I love you and the baby like you were my own, so be careful. I don't want to see you or that baby hurt...And I don't want my son to get in no trouble..." She got up from the chair. She picked Azariah up from the bouncer and kissed her. "She is so cute. How much does she weigh now?"

"She's twelve pounds nine ounces."

"My baby is getting up there. Is she sleeping all night?"

I shook my head no.

"I'll bring a box of baby rice over. Put a tablespoon per ounce in and she'll sleep through the night."

On her way out the door she said, "You think I'm a fool. You and Jay are more than just some friends. Stay in prayer baby. God got a way of making things turn around for the good...."

I smiled and shut the door behind her. Mrs. Duncan kept her word about the cereal, however she sent Jay to deliver it instead. He was holding the baby while I was making her bottles.

"So, have you talked to your dad lately?" He asked

"Yes Sir...He calls twice a week. He got the pictures of the baby and me. I told him I would be up to see him as soon as we were cleared to travel by the doctor. Did you check out her eyes? They turned green."

I was told that my dad had eyes that changed colors and from the looks of it Azariah had taken after him.

"She's going to make me knock somebody out one day." He said smiling down at her.

"That will be my job." A voice said. We both turned our direction towards the door. It was Lorenz; I didn't notice him come in.

He took Azariah from Jay. They glared at each other. Jay backed away and gathered his things.

"I'll talk to you later Sasha."

I nodded my head and I continued making bottles in silence. He gave me a hard stare and took the baby in the room with him. I made sure the baby was bathed and fed, and I put her to bed. I was in my bedroom slipping into my pj's, and I noticed him on his cell phone whispering. I crept in to try to hear.

"I like that. Yeah...That's it." He was stroking his dick and talking on the phone. "Ooh baby right...I miss that sweet pussy...Let me taste that sweet sauce…."

Yuck...He was really into it, making facial expressions and everything. I snuck up behind him grabbed the phone and threw it. He jumped up dick dangling...And he slapped me dead in my face...I was stunned. He hit me. I couldn't believe it. He grabbed me by my neck.

"You interrupted my call now you can finish it for me." He was out of control. He pushed me on the floor. I tried to grab something and hit him...He grabbed my arm and twisted it. I tried to scream, but he held his hand over my mouth.

"Are you gonna be good? I'll let your arm go if you can be good." He pulled me to my knees and pushed my head onto the pillows of the couch...He pulled my panties down.

I was frantic.

"You can't do this...I just had a baby, I'm not healed."

"Bitch shut that shit up. You didn't even have vaginal birth...Plus you ain't bleeding. What I can't get no pussy from my wife now? Or have you been giving it away to the lawyer guy. I'm not stupid Sasha, I know you're fucking him."

"This is rape, your raping me!"

I tried to squirm away from him. The more I squirmed the deeper he pushed my face into the pillow. I felt faint due to a large amount of air being cut off.

He smacked me in the back of the head. "You can't rape your wife dumb ass."

He yanked my legs apart, placed himself between them and

entered me with great force. I let out a small cry as his dick tore through my opening repeatedly.

"You like that don't you bitch! Is that how my dad used to fuck you?"

He smacked me in the head again and picked up his pace. I cried out loud as his pounded away in me showing no mercy.

"Is it? Answer me you dirty bitch, you like that don't you. You like to be treated like a whore, like your scandalous mom. I should have listened to my dad when he told me you weren't shit, but no I had to give you the benefit of the doubt. I loved you, Sasha…and you betrayed me. I went against my flesh and blood for you…and you run off and do this to me!"

I was lost for words. His grip tightened around my neck as he came to an orgasm. Once he was done he collapsed on my back and laid there.

I wanted him to get off but his dick was still inside me pulsating while draining his fluids into me. Moments later he rose up and sat on the couch.

"Now go fix me something to eat..."

I couldn't move, I just cried. He jumped back up came up behind me and grabbed my hair. "I said fix me something to eat..."

"Lorenz please stop. You're hurting me!" I cried.

"Ok, we'll just do it the hard way!" He pulled me by my hair and dragged me to the kitchen.

"Stand the fuck up before I really hurt your dumb ass!"

At this point, I didn't know what he was capable of so I hurried to my feet to avoid more punishment. Pain shot between my legs when I stood up. I covered my mouth to cover my cries. He mushed my head against the cabinet. I grabbed my head as pain rang through it. I couldn't hold it any longer I began to cry out in agony. He smiled in satisfaction picked up his cell phone, and laid on the couch. I limped over to the freezer and pulled out a pack of steak-ems and began to cook for him.

"Hey Baby...Yeah every thing's cool." He sat on the couch and propped his feet on the table.

He sneered at me and said, "Sasha, Shelly says what's up...."

***

The weekend seemed as if it would never end. I couldn't wait until he left. I was in the tub soaking. He was on the phone talking with Shelly and holding the baby. That phone stayed glued to his ear. We had just finished going through another boxing match. This made the second time in three days. Thank God he was leaving in a few hours. I looked at my reflection on the shower door. The bruises were just about gone from the other night, but now I had fresh whelps on my legs.

Earlier the phone had rang...I answered it. It was my dad. I didn't know that he had picked up the phone in the bedroom. He listened in on our whole conversation. When I hung up he was standing behind me scowling. I tried to move away from him, but he grabbed my arm.

"Why would you talk to him after what he did to my mother?"

I snatched my arm away with boldness and went to the bassinet. I doubted if he would attack me while I was holding his precious daughter. I picked up Azariah and held her tightly in my arms.

"That was a mistake and you know it. He was aiming at your father." I know I shouldn't have said that, but I was getting tired of hearing it...

"So that makes it ok? So you saying he should have killed my dad instead?" He began to come towards me with rage in his eyes.

I stood there and played with the baby like I didn't hear him.

"So...now you're ignoring me?" He pushed the end table over.

Ignoring his erratic behavior, I carried the baby in her room and locked the door behind us. I stayed in there with her until she fell asleep. I sat in there for over an hour hoping he had calmed down.

I opened the door and peeked in the living room, I didn't see him. I went in the kitchen to grab the cordless phone. I almost had it in my hand, before he knocked it off the wall.

"You know what your behavior is unacceptable...I think you

are a manic depressant. You need help." I backed away from him. He had something behind his back.

"So, you want to try and diagnose me now?" He moved his hand from behind him. Whack! He had hit me on the leg with the blind turner...I grabbed my leg and tried to run to Azariah's room. He grabbed the back of my robe and pulled me down...

"You want to talk to your daddy? I'm your fucking daddy, and you've been bad."

I clawed at the rug trying to grip it to crawl away from the madman. All attempts to escape were ended when I felt the constant sting of the plastic stick whipping across my flesh. I held my hand over my mouth and took the abuse; I didn't want to startle the baby. Next thing you know he had his pants down getting his pussy, as he would put it. I just laid there as he violated me.

I couldn't believe this was the same man who gave me that beautiful engagement ring, who showered me with flowers, and who couldn't live without me. What went wrong? I know we both messed up. The news of Greg and I sleeping together must have pushed him over the edge. I have seen this happen with so many of my patients. They would reach a breaking point and snap. I had to get out of this, but I knew he wouldn't make it easy.

Now I am sitting here in this water praying, praying that God makes this man disappear out of my life. Deep inside I wished Azariah was *really* Greg's baby. I was in deep meditation when I heard the bathroom door open. It was him. He sat on the toilet and reached for my hair. I flinched when he reached and he touched me.

"Hey, I'm not gonna hurt you. I've been under a lot of stress these last few months. I didn't mean to hurt you...I just...I think I do need to talk to someone."

There was a look of sincerity on his face, one of the old Lorenz I fell in love with. I wasn't falling for it. Not after the beatings he put on me over the last few days.

"I thought that was what Shelly was for...She said at the hospital that she was helping you through your difficult times."

He snickered and the cockiness came back almost

immediately.

"Oh believe me she is...She's a lot of help...Sometimes more help than I can handle." He bragged. "Well let me get out of here I got a long drive ahead ofme."

He turned back around, "By the way, don't go and get no PFA behind my back...if you do, I promise I will kill you…"

Chapter 31

Memorial Day

Jay picked us up for the church barbecue. I wore a long jean skirt and a Baby Phat t-shirt. Azariah had on a little pink Roca Wear outfit with booties. It was sagging on her, but Jay wanted to see her in it. I was quiet most of the ride. He asked if I was ok. I told him everything was fine. When we got to the house everyone crowded around the baby and Mrs. Duncan took her in the house. She was fussing about germs and it being too early for us to be out. She made me promise to stay indoors, because she didn't want me to have a setback.

Everybody gazed at the baby and couldn't get over her eye color. One of the little boys said she looked like a cat. Everybody laughed. Jay hung out with his Frat brothers most of the day. His mom told him to have fun; she would make sure I was fine. My cell phone had rung and it was my sister Xiomara.

"Hey girl...What's up?" I said.

"Bored as hell! You talk to Papi today?" She asked.

"No... Why, everything Ok?"

"Yes...they moved him to minimum security. You know that means he's on his way out right?"

"Oh my God that is good! I was going to take Azariah to see him when our six weeks were up."

"Really, great what are you doing today? You at a cook out?"

"Yes. I'm with Jay at the church picnic."

"Oh, I see... Did you get that kiss yet?" She laughed.

"Girl shut up... You are a trip. What are you doing with yourself are you working or anything?"

"No...I'm not working right now. I am collecting unemployment...Why, you got a job for me?"

"Yeah right...Like you would move down here" I thought about it for a moment. That would be a great idea.

"When do the girls get out of school?"

"They're out. They go to a charter school. They got out last week. They are in Atlanta for the summer with their grandma."

"Would you like to come here for a while and keep me company?"

I didn't want to be alone with him anymore, especially after the death threat. He was scarring me.

"Girl when? I'm down with that. Are there any cute men at that church of yours?"

"You are so crazy! Will you be ready to come by Wednesday? I can have a plane ticket ready."

"Girl...I'm there. I'll tell Aunt Rosa to check my mail and send me my checks...Jehaida is going to be jealous...Didn't nobody tell her to have all those bad ass kids."

"Ok girl, I'll call you tomorrow with the details. Luv ya sis."

"Luv ya back, Girlie."

I hung up. *I bet he won't try to put his filthy hands on me now*. I said to myself.

I didn't notice Jay beside me. "What did you just say?" He demanded.

His mother was staring me dead in my face. She handed the baby to one of the sisters at the church. She pulled me by the arm to her room. Jay was right on her tracks. She quietly shut the door. She held my face in her hands.

"Jesus...I knew it was a bruise." She said. Jay was pacing back and forth.

I sat there ashamed.

"Sasha sweetie, what's going on?" She asked. "I don't want to cause any trouble. I don't want anyone to call the police. It's not going to happen again." I pleaded.

"What else did he do?" She asked. I pulled my skirt up to show her my legs and thighs.

"Oh Lawd...Jesus!" She exclaimed.

Jay rubbed his hand on the bruises and my leg jumped because they were still in pain.

"What did he hit you with?" He shouted.

"Jay shhh! Please don't, I'm ok. I fixed it. It's not going to happen again."

Jay was furious.

"I know it's not going to happen again. I'm going to make sure that shit don't happen again."

"James Darius Duncan! You better watch your mouth in my sanctified home!" shouted Mrs. Duncan.

"Jay, please promise me you won't do anything. I will fix it. It's not going to happen again. He's not going to be around long. He has a girlfriend. He's seeing Shelly."

"Divorce him!" He shouted. "You got enough proof. Get rid of him. He's done enough to you. I would never hurt you Sasha...I love you...I can take care of you and Azariah. I'll adopt her." He held me in his arms.

I felt tears falling on my skin.

Mrs. Duncan sat on the bed praying.

"Jay, I can't divorce him; not yet anyway. Please don't do anything. Give it time."

"I can't promise you that…." He said softly as he held me in his arms.

***

Later that night, Jay drove me home and walked me in the apartment. He helped me put Azariah to bed. I put the chain lock on the door. I didn't need any more surprises. We laid on the couch talking.

"Xiomara is coming on Wednesday. She's going to stay with me for a while...I don't think he'll try anything with her here."

He was silent. He wrapped his arms around me. The phone rang. I looked on the caller ID, it said Starla Connors.

"Hello."

She was whispering, "Sasha, this is Starla. Do you have a fax machine?"

"Yes... Why? What's wrong?"

"Give me the number... I need to send you something. I will call you tomorrow when I am out of the house to tell you the rest."

She hung up.

I went to the fax machine and waited for the fax. Moments later it came through. I couldn't believe what I was reading...

Jay came over to the fax machine. He read a few lines then took it out of my hands.

"Can you believe that shit?" I yelled.

He held his hand out to tell me to hold on. He continued to read it. I put my hand on my head and sat on the edge of the couch. After a few minutes Jay walked over to me.

"You know we are going to have to report this...how did she get a hold of this anyway? This is confidential."

"I have no idea. She told me she would call me tomorrow with the details." I sighed in disbelief. "I can't believe that someone rigged Greg's car."

Jay sat next to me. "But the question is who did it? It could have been Lorenz or Camille. Or maybe even the Shelly girl. She was hanging around them too right?"

I was clueless. I would have said no it couldn't have been Lorenz, but after his behavior this weekend, I couldn't put nothing past him anymore.

"Well, what do we do?" I asked.

"We can sleep on it and we'll figure it out tomorrow." I went to my room and Jay started to make the sofa up for him to sleep.

"Jay, you don't have to sleep on the couch. You can sleep with me…I don't bite." He smiled and followed me to the room.

The next day we sat around the apartment waiting for Starla's call. The phone rang. I answered it on the first ring. It was Xiomara. I talked to her long enough to give her flight information and we said our goodbyes. Two hours later Starla finally called.

"Hey Starla...Where are you?"

“I'm at the mall sitting in Starbucks.”

“How did you get the police report?”

“Commissioner Bradley's step-daughter is my best friend. She told me she walked in on him and my mother a few times. One night when her mom was away she heard them talking about Greg and Mr. Bradley told her he had taken care of everything. She said he copied something for her, and then she left with the paper in her hand. She waited for him to leave out and she went in the copier and found the original document. She held it until I came home from school and she gave it to me.”

“Starla why would she give you something that could harm her family?” I asked.

She paused.

“Sasha you have to promise you won't say anything until I can get her out of his house...”

“Starla...I don't know this is a serious matter...”

“You have to promise me. I am trying to help everybody, he is hurting her and she needs this to come out as much as you do...”

I was concerned. “How is he hurting her?”

“He's fucking her. And he threatens to kill her mom...If she says something...I mean he is the police commissioner. I'm pretty sure he can hide it, the same way he is covering for my mom...”

“Ok Starla, we will do this your way...Do you still have the original?”

“Yes, it has the seal and everything. I mailed it to you today.

Please help us, Sasha. I'll call you soon.”

I promised her and hung up.

I explained everything to Jay. He told me he was going to handle this, but he agreed we had to be careful...for the little girl's sake....

Chapter 32

Sasha

Today, I had my six week check up. My incision had healed correctly, and I was given a clean bill of health. Mrs. Duncan had Azariah for the day, so Xiomara and I decided to go to Bojangles' for lunch. I loved their dirty rice. We ordered our food, and found a place to sit. Xiomara's phone rang, it was Chuck. Chuck was Jay's Frat brother; he had taken her out on a date a few times since she's been here.

While she chatted with him I decided to call Jay. I needed to know if he had found anything else out about the police report.
A few weeks had passed since Starla gave us the vital information surrounding Greg's death. We received the original documents a few days after the fax. Jay thought it would be best if we didn't open it just yet. He wanted to wait until everything came out in the open and then we would hand the unopened letter to the proper authorities. We didn't want to risk being charged with harboring information. I had been anxious since then. I was ready for Camille to get what she deserved.

Jay didn't pick up the phone, so I left a message for him to call me when he had time. Xiomara was still running her mouth with Chuck. I guess she forgot I was here. I thought I better give Lorenz a call. He didn't come home this weekend at all. He claimed he had some type of mandatory conference at the hospital. It really didn't make me any difference. I was to the point I couldn't stand to be in his presence. I personally believe the real reason why he is staying away is because of Xiomara. She had been there for three weeks now. I remember when he came home that weekend after he beat me. She and I were playing cards. He looked as if he could have shit a brick when he saw her. He walked past us as if we weren't there, and went directly to the bedroom. Later that night when I went to bed, he was whispering on the phone to his woman. I turned over and went to sleep.

The next day, I was in Azariah's room getting her dressed, he asked me how long would she be here. I told him indefinitely, he stormed out the house. He didn't come home that following weekend. When he did finally show up, he dropped off a few outfits from Saks 5th Avenue. He informed me that Shelly picked them up while she was in New York. He picked the baby up and carried her over to the mirror and looked at their reflection. I tried to act as if I didn't notice what he was doing. After being in a trance for fifteen minutes, he laid her back down and left.
Reluctantly, I dialed his number. It rang five times and I was about to hang up.

"Hello...Hello," A female answered.

"Yes, who am I speaking with?" I asked.

"Oh...Hey Sasha...this is Shelly, Lorenz is in the shower. Is everything ok with the baby?"

I couldn't believe this whore...she was real nonchalant about it, like it was cool that my husband was at her house taking a shower.

"Shelly, why is he taking a shower at your house? Why are you answering his phone?" I was irritated.

"Oh girl, this isn't my house this is our condo...didn't he tell you?"

"Tell me what!" I found myself getting a little loud. Xiomara had sat her phone down and looked at me.

"Woo...no need to get upset. I thought you knew we were roommates. My office moved to Baltimore, and we thought it would be more sufficient if we just shared a place. When he gets out the shower I will tell him to give you a call before we go out to lunch. Give my baby a kiss for me." She hung up.

I sat there with my mouth hanging. Xiomara told Chuck she would call him back.

"What's going on Sis? Who was that on the phone?" She asked.

Did she just say give her baby a kiss? Did she just rush me off the phone? I was in shock.

"Girl, Shelly and my husband live together!"

"I told you Sasha, I told you that you needed to handle that shit. I knew it! Where they live, East or West Baltimore. I got people's that will fuck both of them up...Oh my God...I knew that shit…."

She just kept rambling on. I couldn't do anything but laugh. I don't think I was hurt, because deep down inside I already knew it. I just wish he would have told me. What messed me up is that she acted as if that was normal. That it was cool for her to be living with my husband. I looked down at my rice and tried to eat it, but I had lost my appetite. Xiomara packed up her food and said she was ready. I guess she could tell I wasn't trying to be there anymore.

She cursed in Spanglish about the whole situation while we were driving home. Once we got home I did the unimaginable. I went to my room and shut my door. I grabbed my phone.

"Hello," she said sleepily.

"Camille...How long has Shelly been fucking my husband?"

"Miss Sasha...I didn't expect to hear from you. How's what's her name, Alissa, or something like that?" She was trying to be funny.

"Azariah is fine. I asked you a question! How long Camille!"

"Wow, I had no idea they were intimate. I thought she was like his support person, therapist, confidant, you know what I'm trying to say. She's back home in Long Island. I haven't talked to her in a while." She said flatly.

Maybe she really didn't know.

"Oh no...She's not in Long Island. She and my husband live together in Baltimore. She works there now. They share a condo.

They are together!"

"Are you fucking kidding me?" That woke her ass up.

"They are what! Living together...that slimy bitch. That was not supposed to happen!"

So she did know something. "What wasn't supposed to happen?" I demanded.

"Sasha dear...your so called husband and I have been sleeping together ever since the night of the funeral. Shelly came here to visit while I was away in Dallas. She was supposed to come to help him through his difficult time. I mean his father had just died. Then you abandoned him, and then he gets crushed when he finds out you slept with his father, and his precious Arissa may have not been his. He was on the verge of a breakdown and the bitch seduced him.

"My baby's name is Azariah, and you can't blame this shit on me, Camille! You are a dirty deceitful bitch. How about you do us all a favor and slit your fucking wrist, because life as you know it is about to be over!" I banged in her ear.

Xiomara came in. "Girl is everything Ok? Who was that! Was it that bitch Shelly?"

I couldn't say anything. I felt like I was dying inside. All the lies, treachery, and revenge; all of it was getting to me. I was starting to think if it was worth it. I wanted to vomit, vomit all of it out of me...

***

Back in Baltimore…

Shelly

I felt bad when I hung up the phone. I mean I didn't hate Sasha or anything, she just happened to be in the way. I erased her number off the caller ID. There was no need for him to know she called. He had grown to hate her anyway. I walked into the bathroom and gazed at the beautiful black Adonis in my shower. The water glistened on his smooth chocolate skin; I became jealous of the suds that ran down his strong calves. I wanted to slide my lips around that thick beam of his. I felt myself getting moist. I had to keep my composure; he had a meeting to get to. I would have plenty of time to jump on that later. I went into the living room and turned on the flat screen. I flicked through the channels; nothing interesting was on as usual. I changed it to CNN. I knew something entertaining would pop up on here sooner or later. Lorenz came out the bedroom with just a towel on. Damn, he looked good. I was lying on the couch with just my thong on. I hated wearing clothes. He didn't mind he always told me it was easy access and besides he loved looking at my big ass and tits. I know he did, because Sasha's ass was most definitely big. She was a big girl period. Not obese, but if she turned down a few meals it wouldn't kill her. I could see what he saw in her. She was a sweet person, a little sneaky, but sweet. She was also very pretty. She had nice hair, her skin was flawless, but she wasn't what he needed. I was.

"Did my phone ring?" He asked.

"No baby, it was the TV." I lied. "You better hurry and get dressed. You're going to be late for your lunch meeting."

He waved me off and went back into the bedroom. Moments later he came out looking hotter than ever. He had on his charcoal Ralph Lauren suit. I wanted to just eat him up. He walked over to me and stuck his tongue down my throat, I bit his lip. I didn't want to let go.

"Mmm", I moaned.

I grabbed at his bulge in his pants. He squeezed my tit, and grabbed his phone.

"We'll finish this later...Be good." He said and walked out the door.

I ran my hand over my breasts.

You damn right we will finish this later....

I went over to the window to watch him walk to his truck. He looked up at me and blew me a kiss, and drove off. Damn, I loved that man. I can't believe he will soon be all mine. My thoughts were interrupted by my phone.

Damn, who is this? I looked at the caller ID. *Oh shit, what does this bitch want*!

"What Camille!"

"*YOU STINKIN LOW DOWN BITCH! WHAT THE FUCK*

ARE YOU DOING IN BALTIMORE?"

I had to stop her in her tracks.

"First of all honey, don't call me with your voice raised. I'm a fucking adult and you talk to me with respect! You know I will whip your ass right?" I had to be direct, because that bitch was getting out of hand,

She got cocky.

"Oh don't go doing that big, bad, New York chick shit on me. You won't put your hands on me because if you do, I'll tell him how you're trying to take him for his money! But you need to remember he is married and whatever he has goes to his wife and that kid."

She was pissing me off, because she thought she knew everything. She didn't know the half of it.

"Won't shit go to her ass, she's cheating on him with that guy, and he is just waiting until he can prove it and then he's divorcing her and taking his baby. We are going to be a family, and you're just mad because he didn't want to be with your washed up ass!"

She began to laugh.

"You are truly delusional. Do you really think he is going to divorce her? Hmmm, I mean really Shellz, he would have done it the minute he found out she was screwing Greg! Baby, what makes you think I would allow you to be with him, I have too much dirt on your ass. I could ruin you. Have you powdered your nose lately?" She busted out laughing.

"I don't do that anymore and you know it." I was heated. I could kill her right know.

"I know you don't do it anymore, but he doesn't know you ever did it period. If you want to keep that and you're other little dirty secrets quiet, you'll get the fuck outta there like yesterday. Bye bitch!"

I sat their flabbergasted.

What was I going to do? I can't let her win; I worked too hard for this.

The more I thought about it the angrier I got. She wasn't getting away with this. I went to my jewelry box, and pulled a key out. I went to the top of the closet, and opened my safe. I opened the envelope and took the pictures out. I smiled to myself. I hated to do this. She's a nice piece of ass, but it was time for this bitch to say goodnight and this would do the trick.

Chapter 33

Sasha

Things had been going quite well lately. Azariah was growing fast, she was about to be two months old in a few days. She had gotten so fat. Her skin complexion finally stayed at one pigment. We didn't know if she was going to be brown skin or what. She brightened up, she was lighter than me. Lorenz didn't like that at all. I tried to tell him, it didn't mean anything. My parents aren't that dark and neither was I. He was really childish with it. That was last week. He just popped up out of nowhere. He was here for about an hour then left.

Xiomara and I were on our way to my house.

"So, how did you get all this money?" She asked. I smiled.

"It's actually Azariah's, she inherited it from her grand-father. He had the house built when he found out I took the job in Chapel Hill. I guess he was trying to look out for his grandchild."

When we pulled up to the house, her mouth hit the floor.

"This is your house! Oh my God, why are you living in that little apartment? This is unbelievable."

I opened the door so she could check it out. She ran through the house like a kid in the candy store. This had been the first time I saw the house furnished. It was breath taking. I couldn't wait until all this was over so I could move in. I went upstairs to the nursery. It was pink and green, my sorority colors. I went to check out the bedroom, dark colors just like I wanted. I think it's sexy; it just sets the mood right. I had to laugh at Jay's color selection. Royal purple, gold, and black…he is such a *dawg*.

I took the back steps to the kitchen area. I gazed up at the fifteen feet high windows. I wonder who he had hang the drapes. Or better yet who would be cleaning those bad boys. Xiomara came up from the basement.

"Yo this is like one of them MTV crib houses. You ain't got to leave here for shit! Are you sure G wasn't slangin dope no more?"

I laughed, "No girl, he owns property. Well not anymore Azariah inherited that too. So if you decide you want to stay here I can get you a job. What are your skills?"

"I worked at a few banks in the credit department, but they were temp jobs. I also did human resources for the state, but I resigned… they were petty."

"Well have you ever thought about going back to school?"

"She wrinkled her nose. "Schools not for me…"

I told her the building I lived in we owned. I asked her if she could handle being a property manager. My old one was leaving in August, and could train her. She gave me a hug and said she didn't really want to go back to Delaware anyway.

I called Jay and told him the news when we were back at the apartment. He was happy to hear it. He told me that he was going to Virginia Beach for the holiday weekend with his boys. He wanted to take me out for dinner the night before he left. I told him it was cool.

"I love you", he said before hanging up.

A warm smile formed across my face. He made a habit of expressing his feelings to me every chance he got. I appreciated that. I believe he was sincere. I sorted through the mail on the table. Someone had sent me Express mail; it was most likely the birth certificate. I just sat it aside. I can't believe how peaceful it was. I wish everyday could be this way....

***

Shelly

I paced back and forth in the living room. I have to do this. I tried to get my mind right.

What if he turns on me? What if he thinks the pictures are a fake? No...He won't. It's too much evidence. Plus I don't have a reason to lie about it.

I looked at the clock, it was 7p.m. He will be here in five minutes. My stomach was doing somersaults. I was about to vomit. I hurried into the bathroom, and hurled. Damn, I hate this shit.

When will it be over?

I wanted a drink bad. But I had to stay focused.

I heard the keys in the door. I ran out the bathroom and placed the envelope on the table. He always puts his keys there. So I know he'll see it. I plopped down on the couch in the nick of time. I closed my eyes and acted as if I was sleep.

Lorenz took off his jacket, threw it on the chair, stood in front of the table dropped his keys, and his eyes went directly to the envelope. I opened one eye and watched him open the package. My stomach started to bubble again. I closed my eyes as tight as I could. I didn't hear anything...Wait a minute...I heard a soft whimper. Was he really crying?

"NO...NO!" He cried. I jumped up. He took the table and threw it across the room. I jumped off the couch.

"Renzo baby! What's wrong?" I was scared. "Calm down. What is it?"

"YOU KNEW ABOUT THIS!" He shouted. He seemed as if he were demon possessed. I backed away from him into the wall.

"I knew what! Baby what are you talking about? What is that in your hand?" I was shaking all over. He took the pictures and pushed them in my face.

"DID YOU KNOW SHE DID THIS...DID YOU KNOW SHE CAUSED THE ACCIDENT!"

I looked at the pictures. There was Camille in the hotel parking lot, while Commissioner Bradley cut the break line on Greg's car.

"Oh...Oh my God...baby...I didn't know! I felt myself getting sick...I tried to hold it down, but it all came up, all over the plush carpet. I fell to my knees as I heaved. He rushed to me.

"Baby tell me you had nothing to do with this!" I was relieved. He didn't think I knew about it.

"I love you...We are going to be a family...I would never hurt you...Camille and Sasha hurt you not me...I always loved you...Camille tried to keep you away from me. She told me she was going to marry you so she could get your money. I don't want any money; I want us to be a family." I cried.

He got up.

"I know you love me...I know you do...It's those BITCHES...THEY DID THIS TO ME...THEY DID THIS SHIT TO MY DAD...THEY DESTROYED HIM." He punched the wall.

I sat in the corner of the room. I was scared. I never saw him this way. I didn't know what to do. He was talking to himself and hitting himself in the head. The phone rang. He took and pulled the cord out the wall. He came over to me with the cord in his hand. I screamed.

"DON'T HURT ME RENZO...IT'S NOT ME IT'S CAMILLE! I DIDN'T DO IT!"

He stared at me with the cord in his hand breathing hard. I thought his heart was going to come out his chest. I got up slowly. I had to distract him, so I did what I do best. I stripped down until I was completely naked.

That should do the trick.

I inched over to him. When I got close enough, I wrapped my arms around his neck.

"Baby I love you. I'm the only one who ever loved you."

I rubbed my body against his. I felt his muscles relax. I ran my tongue over his lips until he opened his mouth. He responded back. He picked me up and carried me into the room. He laid me on the bed. He kissed my breasts and my thighs. I began to moan. Just when I thought things were under control. I felt a horrible pain as if my head was being banged between two iron frying pans. Then everything went dark.

***

Camille

I am so bored. I need some excitement in my life.

I was home alone as usual. Starla was staying the night with one of her little friends. Her attitude has gotten better since that dreadful display in the kitchen. She swore to me that she would never talk about anything she knew concerning Greg's death again. Of course I had to promise her I would not send her back to that school. That reminded me I need to check into a few private schools in my area for her.

I guess it will be cool to have her around especially since everyone had abandoned me. A reminder flashed up on my TV, one of my favorite Lifetime movies was about to come on. I hit the button so I could tune in.

I couldn't believe that it was 10p.m. already. Time flies when you're having fun...not. I was just about to get comfortable when I heard a car pull up in the driveway.

Hmm. I wonder who that could be. I thought. *I know damn well it better not be that damn Pete Bradley.*

I saw his ass last night. I couldn't stand fucking him. He had a little pink dick; I swear it was only four inches. He would turn beet red while we were fucking. He wanted me to make noises and tell him he was the best fuck I ever had. Truth is I always had to be drunk as hell to let him touch me. I walked over to the window to investigate. A big smile came upon my face.

Well…Well if it isn't the prodigal son!

I knew his ass would be back. I ran back over to the couch. I didn't want him to know I saw him coming. I had to put on a front. I heard him come in. I tried to act like I was into the TV. He walked in the living room. He stood in front of me breathing heavy like a savage beast about to attack his prey. It kind of turned me on. I wondered what his issue was. Probably more issues with that *Sasha*. I turned the TV off. I stood up and wrapped my arms around him.

"Baby, I knew you would come back to me."

Instead of showing me affection, he grabbed me by my throat.

"I guess you didn't think I would find out!" He hissed.

He threw me down on the couch.

"What! What the hell are you talking about? Find out about what?" He slapped me across the face.

I was stunned. I tried to get up and defend myself. But he pinned me back down on the couch.

"GET OFF ME! Are you fucking crazy?"

I scratched at his arms...this time he punched me in my head. I stopped fighting him and held my head in pain.

"You see this!"

He put pictures in my face. I tried to focus in on them.

Oh shit! Where did he get them from?

I knew I had to escape. Who knows what he would do to me since he knew the truth. I tried to break free, but I was stuck.

"Lorenz, let me explain...I didn't mean for that to happen...it was meant for Sasha...I thought she had his car...she was trying to ruin our family...she was bre--"

He punched me again this time in my mouth. I screamed at the sight of the thick red blood that began to pour from my mouth.

"Stop lying, Camille...you knew what you were doing. You wanted me...right...?" He was talking real calm and it was frightening.

"Please don't...don't do anything you'll regret. I'll turn myself in...Just please don't hurt me!" I begged. He taunted me.

"I know Ms. Camille ain't begging for mercy." He grabbed me by my hair and dragged me off the couch. My face was near his ankle I reached for it and bit down.

"Oh shit"...he yelled. He let go of my hair and I tried to run. I started screaming for help. He grabbed the back of my shirt and yoked me back. He planted me against the wall and started to choke me...

"BITCH YOU GONNA DIE TONIGHT! YOU USED MY DAD! YOU USED ME...YOU EVEN USED THAT BITCH SASHA! YOU WORTHLESS BITCH! I KNOW ABOUT THE MONEY! SHELLY TOLD ME EVERYTHING! I WOULD HAVE NEVER MARRIED YOU!"

I made my body go limp and held my breath. He thought I was gone, and he let me fall to the floor. I laid there for a minute.

When he got a few feet away I jumped up and grabbed the vase, I ran behind him to hit him, but he caught it and threw me into my 150 gallon aquarium. Glass shattered everywhere hitting me in the face, and all throughout my body. He kicked me in my rib cage several times. I felt blood coming up my throat. He pulled his dick out and pissed on me. Water and fish were hitting my face. I couldn't move.

"One down and one more to go"...he said.

"Don't hurt her…" I whispered. My last thoughts were Sasha...God help her.

Chapter 34

The next day…
Sasha

"You know I'm going to call you every day right?" Jay asked.

We were sitting in the parking lot of my complex. He had me blushing. Our dinner date had ended. Jay was leaving in the morning for Virginia Beach.

"I'm going to miss you, too" I replied, "Just don't do anything you'll regret." I teased.

"You don't have to worry about that...I'm waiting for you." He winked. "Do you want me to walk you to your door?"

"No baby...it's getting late and I know you have to get an early start tomorrow. Go home and get some rest." I gave him a quick hug and turned to get out the car.

"Wait. Don't go just yet…"

I turned back to him. He gently pulled my face towards his and planted his lips on mine. My body quivered. His thick tongue forced its way through my lips. I was in bliss. This was all too familiar. I pulled away. He didn't understand.

"Sasha...I'm sorry, I didn't mean to be disrespectful." He said embarrassed.

"No baby, I wanted you too, but we have to do this the right way this time." I kissed him softly on the lips. "Call me to let me know you made it home safely."

"I love you, Sasha."

"I know...I know you do..." I said and shut the door. When I got into my building I gave him the ok to leave. I stood there for a moment and watched him drive off.

I love you too.

I hated going back to an empty bed. I climbed the stairs to my apartment, and fantasized about being with Jay. Mrs. Duncan had Azariah, and Xiomara was on a date. I knew she wasn't home yet it was too early. I checked my watch, it was only nine o'clock. I reached my door and stuck the key in to unlock it. To my surprise the door was already open. I guess she was home after all.

I went in and it was pitch dark in the house. I went to turn the hall light on and jumped!

"Oh shit!" Lorenz was standing right in front of me. "Damn, you scared me." I said walking pass him. I sat my purse on the counter and went over to check my caller ID. He was right behind me. I ignored him. It showed Camille's number like ten times. I sucked my teeth. That chick just doesn't give up. She called my cell phone earlier today. I didn't even answer. I just pushed the end call button.

I turned away from the phone and he was right there. I was getting frustrated.

"What do you want? I don't have time for this. I'm tired and I'm ready to go to bed." I tried to push past him. He wouldn't budge.

"Come on I'm not playing."

"Sasha...you know I love you right?" He asked.

Oh here we go I thought.

"Well you have a poor way of showing it."

He let me pass. I went to the kitchen to get a bottle of water. He watched my every move. He was starting to freak me out.

"You look very pretty tonight. Where did you go?" He asked.

"Does it matter?" I said coldly. "My name is not Shelly...you need to ask her what she is doing. That's your *wifey.*" I opened the bottle to take a drink. He came over to where I was standing. He stood behind me and lifted up the back of my dress and began rubbing my thighs and kissing my neck.

"Stop Lorenz! What? You and Shelly going through something?"

He moved his hands to my ass and began to massage it, and kiss my ears. My coochie started to thump. He knew that was my spot. I needed to end this before things got too far. I sat the bottle down and tried to move his hands.

"Lorenz, you need...to...stop."

His hands made their way to my spot and began to play with her. Oh shit...it was feeling good.

"Stop...you...need to stop"...my protest was weakening.

He dropped to his knees, pulled down my panties, and spread my cheeks with one hand. He was still working the pussy with the other. I felt his tongue plunge between my cheeks. I came instantly. I tried to get it together; I hate this man. He put me through so much...but he was making me feel so good.

He stood up and lifted me on the kitchen table. He dropped his pants and stroked his dick. I had to admit, I did miss my old friend. I just hated who he was attached to. He spread my legs apart and slowly slid my friend deep inside. I closed my eyes and decided I would enjoy the ride one last time.

He worked me slow, grinding deep in me. I felt electricity run through my veins. This was the old Lorenz I missed. I kept my eyes closed and imagined us how it used to be, but that didn't work. Thoughts of him and Shelly came in my mind; I thought about Camille, I thought about how he abused me.
I came to my senses immediately.

"Stop! I can't do this."

I tried to get up. He pushed me back and continued doing his thing.

"No, I need you to stop! Now!"
He stopped, but he didn't pull out.

"What's wrong? You don't want me to make love to you?" He tried to sound all-innocent. "Don't you love me?"

"No...I don't love you. Truth is I don't think I ever did!" I wanted to hurt him.

He pulled out of me and pulled his pants up. He looked as if he was hurt. Mission accomplished. I got off the table and fixed myself.

"I mean really...I believe we were just caught up. We started off wrong...we didn't even know each other. Everything was a big secret. You can't build a life off of secrets and lies." He just stood there.

I walked up to him...and touched his arm. He snatched away.

"Lorenz, don't be that way, we just need to end this. You can have a life with Shelly or Camille or whoever. You can still see Azariah. She's too young to even know what divorce is."

He shook his head, "That's not going to work Sasha. We took a vow...and we said until death do us part. Shelly was right about you, about all of you! Camille had to learn the hard way. I tried not to go there with you. I wanted to try and work it out one last time. All you bitches are alike!" He snapped.

"You know what...leave...just leave Ok. I can see where this is getting ready to go." I went to the bedroom and began emptying out his drawers.

"If you don't file...Then I will...I feel trapped. I need to be free." I said. "I want to start a new life." I looked in the mirror in front of me and he was behind me. Not saying a word.

I turned around. "We were just never meant to be...face it."

There was nothing but silence between us. We just stared each other down. I didn't feel safe anymore. I was used to him running off at the mouth, or trying to put his hands on me. His silence was frightening. I slowly turned around and shut the drawer. I knew I shouldn't have turned my back on him. That's when he made his move. I saw his reflection in the mirror as he charged at me. I quickly turned around towards him and covered my face.

He pushed me against the mirror. The back of my head crashed into it. Thank God it didn't break. It just cracked. He tried to wrap his hands around my neck, but I managed to kick him off me. I ran to the closet and pulled out a baby Louisville slugger.

Xiomara gave it to me just in case he decided to act up again. I bashed him in the head with it several times, but he kept coming. I ran out the room, but he was hot on my tracks. I went to the kitchen and grabbed the phone. I dialed Jay's number. When it started ringing I dropped the phone and ran towards the door. I tried to open it, but he slammed it shut and pushed me into the wall.

"HELP! SOMEBODY HELP ME!" I screamed from the top of my lungs. His right fist slammed into the side of my nose and blood gushed everywhere. I covered my face, to block the blows that he was throwing on me.

"YOU RUINED ME! YOU FUCKING RUINED ME! I LOVED YOU...I WANTED TO SPEND...MY...LIFE... WITH...YOU BUT...YOU...HAD TO...GO...AND...BE A SLUT LIKE YOUR MOTHER...GET THE FUCK UP..."

I didn't budge...I was so woozy...I couldn't see straight...Blood was running all in my mouth. I was tired. I just wanted him to kill me and get it over with...

"Just...kill...me." My voice was faint.

"What did you say?"

"Just fucking kill me! You hate me so much! Take the baby! I'm tired..."

He stood there for a few seconds with a confused look on his face. He bent down to my ear and whispered, "I love you."

He kissed my bloody lips and wrapped his hands gently around my throat and applied pressure. I closed my eyes and waited to drift away.

Within seconds his grip was gone...I tried to catch my breath...I heard a bunch of tussling, and punches being thrown...
I remember hearing Xiomara's voice, she was crying,

"Sasha...Oh my God...please don't die...She held me in her arms, please don't die...KILL HIS ASS YALL, CUT HIS FUCKING EVIL HEART OUT! FUCKING KILL HIM!"

A few minutes later I heard more voices.

"EVERYBODY...FREEZE!" The cops had come.

"GET THE MEDICS UP HERE ASAP!"

It was all across the news about Lorenz's rampage, and a police Commissioner who committed suicide outside his home. He was wanted in Delaware for Camille's attempted murder. Somehow they thought the two had a connection. The authorities were notified by the victim's daughter, Starla, he was on his way to Raleigh, N.C. to get me. They went to the wrong address. They thought I was living at my house, in Chapel Hill. Someone else called about a woman screaming from the apartment and when they came to check it out, it was Lorenz doing the screaming.

Chuck and Jay whooped his ass good from what I heard. He was treated at a local hospital. After his arraignment here they were going to ship him to Delaware to face charges. I was lying in the hospital bed recovering from my injuries. My nose was broken in two places and I had a slight concussion. Both of my eyes were black and my face was swollen. Mrs. Duncan came by and prayed with me. Xiomara was home packing my things.

I couldn't bear to go back to that apartment. I was moving into my house as soon as I was released. Jay sat at my side around the clock. I told him to go and enjoy himself; there was no need for him to sit in the hospital on a holiday. He told me he wasn't going anywhere.

I spoke with Starla earlier that day; she said her mother has been heavily sedated. Her face is bandaged because she suffered from extensive lacerations. She told me that a police officer sits outside her mothers' door around the clock because she is being charged with premeditated murder. They found pictures at the scene of her and Commissioner Bradley in the parking lot, and they found a copy of the real police report in her office. Starla told me she was going to live with her aunt in Jersey. I didn't realize Camille had any siblings. She told me it was her dad's sister. She explained her dad's wife wasn't ready to accept her as of yet, but her aunt seemed cool. I told her if she needed anything to call me. She told me thank you before she hung up.

A few days later, I was released from the hospital. Jay and I were enjoying the summer breeze. Xiomara was in the pool with Azariah. I was a little leery about that. She was only two months and she had her in a pool. My face had gone down some, but I had to wear sun glasses because my eyes were still sensitive. Lorenz was sent back to Delaware. I heard he was trying to plead insanity. The sad thing is, since he is a psychologist he just may get away with it.

Chapter 35

Gander Hill Prison...

Lorenz was sent to Gander Hill Prison in Wilmington, Delaware. He thought he was going to a mental institution until his hearing, but there was no space available. The guard took him to his cell and locked the door behind him. He mumbled to himself and kept hitting himself in the head. He wanted them to really think he was crazy. When the officer was out of sight, his show ended. He sat there on his bunk alone.

About twenty minutes later he was accompanied by an inmate in his mid to late 40's. He stood about 6'4"; he was stocky, but very solid. He had a honey brown complexion and green eyes. There was something familiar about this man. He couldn't remember, but it was something about his eyes. The man sat down next to him and pulled out an envelope with pictures. He looked at Lorenz...

"Hey, you want to see my pictures of my family?" The man was attempting to be friendly.

"No, that's alright...I'm not really in the mood for it." Lorenz showed no interest.

The man continued to look through his pictures. He would smile and then laugh out loud in delight.

"You know I am getting out tomorrow. I mean not completely out...I have to do a halfway house...But it's the closest I've been to freedom in almost 31 years." The man said as he looked down and continued going through his pictures.

He continued to ignore the man.

"Do you have any kids?" The man asked.

He figured he better answer the man so he could shut up. "Yeah, I got a daughter. She's a little over two months."

"You miss her?"

"Yeah...I guess...I mean...I don't have a connection with her like that...Her mom makes things difficult." The man moved around like he was a little agitated.

"Well that's a shame. I have three beautiful daughters...I never met one of them though. She just had a baby girl this past May."

Lorenz lifted his head, "My daughter was born in May, too."

"Yeah that is ironic...I bet she was born May 5th."

"Yeah she was...." Lorenz froze.

He finally looked up into the man's eyes. Fear set in immediately. This man had the same eyes as his daughter. He jumped up from the bunk startled by his discovery.

Mixxon flipped a picture over and showed him Sasha and Azariah. "Yeah isn't that ironic?" Mixxon said.

Lorenz tried to throw a punch but Mixxon caught his hand in mid air and punched him in his nose.

"You want to break my daughter's nose? I'm going to break your fucking face." Lorenz fell to the floor.

Mixxon continued to kick him in the face. It looked like the floor and the bottom of Mixxon's boot was playing ping pong with his head. The guard came in.

"That's enough Mixx. Let me get you outta here. I don't want to get you caught up in here." Before Mixxon left, he told Lorenz to get used to the ass beatings. Sasha had a lot of family in here and they knew who he was.

Lorenz continued to be brutalized sexually and physically. Two weeks later a guard came in to check on him, and they found him dead hanging in his cell. They ruled it as a suicide.

I was sad, yet relieved. It was finally over. I received the call early Sunday morning while we were all getting ready for church. When the warden told me I didn't believe it. I wanted to cry, but nothing would come out. Damn...I didn't want him to die. Azariah was lying on my bed. I picked her up and cuddled her.

"He's gone honey." I whispered. "The bad man is gone."

***

The Funeral

I sat on the front pew with Azariah. There were a few people there; Nothing like Greg's funeral. Most of the people were his co-workers from our old job. During the viewing you could hear them whispering how his father must be turning in his grave. Some of them said he suffered a breakdown after his father died. I watched everyone as they walked by his casket. When they were about to close it, a woman who was dressed in an all black designer maternity dress started to make a scene.

"Oh…Renzo...baby...Don't leave me....Oh my beautiful Lorenz...What am I gonna do!"

Then she threw herself on his dead body and rocked the casket. The ushers rushed her and carried her away. She screamed his name as they were carrying her away. Jay refused to come to the service; he sat out in the car. He didn't understand why I needed to be there. I don't think he really understood that I was still his wife. I mean, he needed some type of family there. When the service was about over they asked me if I wanted to do a final viewing. I declined.

The ushers rolled the casket down the aisle. I followed behind it. Everyone was staring at me and gave me smiles and wishes. One woman told me she had much respect for me; she said she didn't think she could be at the man's funeral who tried to kill her. I smiled and kept it moving.

When they were loading him in the hearse, the woman in black was back.

"Please let me see him one more time...Please..."

The usher looked at me...I nodded. They opened it so she could look at him. She wept and kissed his lips.

"It's a boy baby...I'm having your son..." She said. "I'm going to tell him how wonderful his father was."

She backed away crying hysterically.

I went to her. "Hey, Shelly." I planted my hand on her shoulder for comfort. I knew she was hurting. My heart was heavy as well. I would be lying if I said otherwise.

"Sasha...He didn't mean it...He was confused...He didn't deserve this Sasha...My baby doesn't deserve this…."

"Shelly, Azariah won't know him either...She won't have her father."

She knocked my hand from her shoulder and sneered. If looks could kill, Shelly would have been up for murder. She pointed her chunky finger in my face.

"Don't fucking play with me, Sasha. You and I both know that's not his child. I know you have the proof. Camille told me she sent it to you!"

I tensed up a bit. I wasn't aware that she knew the truth. I managed to fake a confident laugh, "Prove it."

I turned to walk away but she grabbed my arm.

"That trust fund belongs to my son. He's the first born! Sasha...you're not being fair." I snatch away from her. *Fair?* She had a lot of nerve to talk about being fair.

"No, that's where you're wrong. I *am* being fair. I gave you everything you deserve...Nothing!" Jay drove up beside us at the right time because by the look of it things were about to get messy. He wore a concerned expression.

"Is everything ok?"

I smiled wickedly as I opened the car door. I took one last look at Shelly before I closed the door for good. She looked deranged. A sense of calm came over me.

"It is now. Have a nice life Shelly."

I closed the door and didn't look back.

"What was that all about?" he asked.

I patted his thigh to reassure him and smiled, "Nothing…nothing at all."

***

My New Beginning...

The following year James and I had a traditional wedding at his father's church. Everything was how it should be; my father gave me away, and all of my family was in attendance, even Starla came through to show her support. Everything was perfect…at least it seemed that way. There was one situation I just didn't know how to fix. Shelly was right. Azariah wasn't Lorenz's child nor was she Greg's for that matter.

Today was my wedding day. I had already selected the perfect gift for my soon to be husband. My gift was the truth; the truth that Azariah was indeed his daughter. I sat at the vanity as they applied my makeup. My mind began to wonder back to that night. The night Greg hurried me off the resort so that he could be with his wife. I was so hurt. My intentions were to leave but I just couldn't, I was tired of running and that night I planned to confront my situation. However that's not how things went down.

I was on my 4th Long Island Ice Tea. I was so done that my body felt numb. I watched everyone dancing and having a good time. Before I knew it tears where streaming down my face.

"It can't be that bad sweetheart," a voice said.

I looked around to see who said something. I was so tore up. I was seeing double.

"Hey, I'm over here."

I looked to my left and there was this guy sitting next to me. I must have gave him a stank look.

"I can leave if you want...I just saw you crying and I didn't think a pretty lady like yourself should be sitting here alone."

I managed to crack a smile.

"Thank you..." I slurred. "So what brings you down here?" I asked.

"I'm on business, right now. One of my clients needed me to close a deal for him, so he paid for my mini vacation."

"Must be nice." I tried to focus to see what he looked like. From what I could see he was good looking. I know his ass sounded good.

"So, what are you getting into tonight?" He asked

I gave a sexy smile. "Hopefully you," I said giving him a little sexy laugh.

"I'm not that kind of guy to take advantage of a lady when she isn't in her right mind."

His sultry voice was turning me on by the minute.

"Oh Sweetie, believe me I'm definitely in my right mind, I just know what I like. Plus, I need to get my mind off a few things and I think you just might do the trick."

After we shared a few more drinks, he whisked me away to his place and it was on and poppin'. That man was awesome in the bed. He was romantic; he licked and sucked every hole on my body. We tore that house up; we did it any and everywhere and kept it going until the wee hours in the morning.

The next morning I found myself lying in the bed alone. I tried to remember what occurred the night before but my memory was shot. I couldn't even remember what he looked like. Maybe it was a dream. I tried to convince myself, but I knew it wasn't. I had to face reality, that I had unprotected sex with a man whose name I didn't even know…

***

Lunch with Mr. Duncan

After I received my food, we sat around talking.

"Sasha...You don't remember me do you?" He took a bite of his food and chewed with a slight smile on his face.

"Remember you from what? I know you were the one who showed me the house." I was puzzled, not sure of what he was getting at.

"You don't remember Key West?" He smiled.

"You know that night at Olivia's; we had our night of blissful sex."

I put the fork on my plate. Then it all came to me. That whole night flashed through my head like a trailer to a motion picture.

I couldn't believe it. It was him. He was the mystery man.

"Not you. That was not you...?" I put my head down in shame.

Here I am trying to play a victim and I had sex fit for a porno with this man and didn't even know his name. He laughed.

"It's Ok...Don't be embarrassed. I wanted to tell you when I first saw you...I was just so shocked about seeing you again. I thought about you so many times since then. That was one incredible night."

I didn't know what to say. "Jay, I'm not like that. So much was going on with me at that time. I can't believe it's you. I tried so hard to forget about that night...I just…I don't know what to say…"

"Oh...ok I got you. My sex must have been trash you didn't even remember our night together...my feelings are hurt," he teased.

"Shut up! It's not like that, from what I do remember it was awesome… I was just so drunk, like I said, I had so many other things going on I kind of blocked it out my mind."

Before Lorenz passed, I received an envelope. So much was going on I really didn't have time to check it out. The day I received the news of his death I opened it. Inside was a document and a letter. I sat down and read the letter. I couldn't believe what I was reading. Then I looked at the document. It was a letter from Camille explaining that she had the paternity test rigged. She sent me a copy of the original documents. It said that it was a 0.00% chance that Lorenz could be the father. They had no genetic compatibility. This meant that Greg was not the father either.

I kept this secret not knowing what our future would be when the truth came out. Azariah would lose everything. It would all end up in Shelly's hand since she truly did have the heir to the Hayward fortune. Through the mirror I could see Azariah. She sat in her little princess chair getting her soft curls twisted in a spiral ponytail. I questioned myself. Was it really necessary for him to know the truth? He already had unconditional love for her. The answer was clear as day. No. My love for Azariah was beyond measure; there was no limit to what I would do to secure her future. I wanted her to enjoy something I never really achieved… true happiness.

***

Three Months Later…

"Sir you asked to see me?" Jay asked as he entered his father's office. Reverend James Duncan senior sat at his desk with his hands folded in front him. He could barely look his son in his eyes. He never imagined that he would have to break the news like this.

"Yes son come in and take a seat." His voice was heavy and sorrow could be heard in his tone.

Jay knew something had to be wrong. He had that worry wrinkle on his forehead. Jay sat in the red velvet cushion chair. He waited for his father to speak first as he always did. They were always taught not to speak unless spoken to and he had kept those rules close to his heart. He had planned to instill the same values into Azariah and his future children. It helped him grow to be the man that he was today.

"Son, I don't know where to start. So I'll start at the beginning. About six years before you were born you know I accepted my calling into the ministry. I was about nineteen years old at the time. I had just married your mother and graduated from the seminary. I was assigned to be an assistant pastor at a church in Aden, North Carolina. It was a little church not much bigger than one of those double wide trailers they have now.
Your mother was just entering her freshman year over at Shaw College in Raleigh. She was going to stay on campus while I was in training. Even though we were married the only time I really got to see her was on the weekends when she would come down to the church. Most people thought we were a little crazy for getting married. They thought she would be tempted by the football players and get caught up in the partying foolishness.
But I wasn't worried about her. I knew I had nothing to worry about and she proved me right." He looked at a picture of her on the desk and smiled.

"There was a pretty young woman who served as my secretary at the church. She was a pretty brown thing; big hips, big thighs, with a big pretty smile, a down home country gal. Her name was Laila. She had just graduated from high school. A lot of men lusted for her but she didn't pay them any mind. She seemed to be interested in doing the Lord's work and that was it.

We had to spend a lot of time together especially when I was sent out to preach at other churches. One night we were at a revival in Federalsburg, Maryland. I had been there for a week. We were supposed to leave that night but my car wouldn't start. We had very little money left so we had to get a room to share at one of the motels in the town. Everything started out to be innocent. I made a cot on the floor and gave her the bed.

Well later that night, I felt something underneath my cover. At first I thought it was a raccoon or possum that got in the room. When I opened my eyes it was Laila. She was doing things to me that only a wife should be doing to her husband. I tried to stop her. But son I'm a man and I am human. I'm not perfect. Things went too far. I know I should have made her stop but it got good to me. Laila and I kept it going on for six months.

The only reason I stopped was because your mother came to me and said she had a dream that I was sleeping with her and she was going to have baby. I tried to deny it. But the hurt in your mother's eyes wouldn't let me lie. I told her the truth and promised that I would end it. But that wasn't enough for your mother. She had me take her to Laila's house so we could confront her together."

Jay sat back in his chair flabbergasted. He couldn't believe what he was hearing. His father the Great Reverend Duncan had stepped out on his mother.

"Dad I don't know what to say. Obviously she took you back because you are still together." Jay said not knowing exactly why his father was telling him this story.

"Yes son she did forgive me. But her dream was right. She was four months pregnant. I just knew my career was over. I thought Laila was going to go straight to the Bishop but she didn't. She only wanted money so she could go and start over somewhere else. We didn't have much to give but your mother had a few dollars saved away for the purchase of our home. She gave her half the money and she disappeared. A few years later, she sent us pictures of the baby. I had a little girl. We sent her money over the years to take care of her and she continued to send me pictures. Then one year it all stopped. I never saw her again until a few months ago. I knew it was her when I laid eyes on her. Now Jay this is where you come in. Your sister is in trouble and she needs help. I need you to help her. We are her family." He went into his desk drawer and pulled out a photograph.

When he handed Jay the picture he jumped out of his seat. "No it can't be!" he shouted.

"Sorry son, it is and she needs you…."

To Be Continued…

So Real You Feel You Lived It!

Street Knowledge Publishing LLC
1902-B Maryland Ave
Wilmington, DE 19805
TOLL FREE: 1.888.401.1114
www.streetknowledgepublishing.com

Date: ____________________

Purchaser ______________________________
Mailing Address ______________________________
City ____________ State ____________ Zip Code ________

Qty.	ISB Number	Title of Book	Price Each	Total
	978-0-9822515-6-0	Bloody Money	$15.00	
	978-0-9822515-9-1	Bloody Money 2	$15.00	
	978-0-9799556-4-8	Bloody Money 3	$15.00	
	978-0-9799556-0-0	Tommy Good story	$15.00	
	978-0-9822515-0-8	Tommy Good Story II	$15.00	
	978-0-9746199-1-0	Me & My Girls	$15.00	
	978-0-9746199-0-3	Cash Ave	$15.00	
	978-0-9822515-1-5	Merry F$$kin' Xmas	$15.00	
	978-0-9799556-0-7	A Day After Forever	$15.00	
	978-0-9822515-3-9	A Day After Forever 2	$15.00	
	978-0-9746199-6-5	Don't Mix the Bitter with the Sweet	$15.00	
	978-0-9799556-9-3	Playing For Keeps	$15.00	
	978-0-9799556-3-1	Pain Freak	$15.00	
	978-0-9799556-5-5	Dipped Up	$15.00	
	978-0-9799556-6-2	No Love No Pain	$15.00	
	978-0-9746199-4-1	Dopesick	$15.00	
	978-0-9799556-7-9	Lust, Love & Lies	$15.00	
	978-0-9746199-7-2	The Queen of New York	$15.00	
	978-0-9746199-8-9	Sin 4 Life	$15.00	
	978-0-9822515-4-6	A Little More Sin	$15.00	
	978-0-9746199-5-8	The Hunger	$15.00	
	978-0-9746199-3-4	Money Grip	$15.00	
	978-0-9822515-7-7	Young Rich and Dangerous	$15.00	
	978-1-944151-26-3	Street Victims	$15.00	
	978-1-944151-28-7	Street Victims II	$15.00	
	978-1-944151-30-3	Street Victimes III	$15.00	
	978-1-944151-32-4	A Small Wonder	$15.00	
	978-1-944151-45-4	Coup De Grace	$15.00	
	978-1-944151-47-8	Burton Boys (May 2017)	$15.00	
	978-1-944151-56-0	Burton Boys 2	$15.00	
	978-1-944151-58-4	Burton Boys 3	$15.00	
	978-1-944151-00-3	Dirty Living	$15.00	
	978-1-944151-65-2	Watch What You Say	$15.00	
		Total Books Ordered	Quantity	
			Subtotal	
SHIPPING/HANDLING (Via U.S. Priority Mail) $7.20 for 1st book, $2.00 for each additional book Institutional Check & Money Orders ONLY (No Personal Checks Accepted)			Shipping Total	
		Total	$	

Street Knowledge Publishing LLC
1902-B Maryland Ave
Wilmington, DE 19805
TOLL FREE: 1.888.401.1114
www.streetknowledgepublishing.com

Date: ____________________

Purchaser ______________________________
Mailing Address ______________________________
City ____________ State ____________ Zip Code ________

Qty.	ISB Number	Title of Book	Author	Price Each	Total
	Butterfly Collection				
		Beautiful Demise	K.D. Harris	$13.99	
		Scarred	K.D. Harris	$13.99	
		Pressure (Coming April 2017)	K.D. Harris	$13.99	
		Dying to Fit In (Coming June 2017)	K.D. Harris	$13.99	
		Legacy (Coming August 2017)	K.D. Harris	$13.99	
		Classy Clique (Coming Sept. 2017)	K.D. Harris	$13.99	
		Caged Secrets (Coming Nov. 2017)	K.D. Harris	$13.99	
		Messy Media (Coming Dec. 2017)	K.D. Harris	$13.99	
	SKP Erotica				
	978-1-944151-04-1	Beyond Measure	K.D. Harris	$15.00	
	978-1-944151-06-5	Beyond Measure II	K.D. Harris	$15.00	
	978-1-944151-62-1	Beyond Measure III (April 2017)	K.D. Harris	$15.00	
	978-1-944151-08-9	The Games We Play	K.D. Harris	$15.00	
	978-1-944151-02-7	For The Love Of It	K.D. Harris	$15.00	
	Eric B Crime Novels				
	978-1-944151-20-1	That Was Dirty	Wasiim	$15.00	
	978-1-944151-22-5	It Gets Dirtier	Wasiim	$15.00	
	978-1-944151-24-9	As Dirty As It Gets	Wasiim	$15.00	
	978-0-9799556-8-6	Money and Murder	Fred Brown	$15.00	
	978-1-944151-35-5	Money and Murder II	Fred Brown	$15.00	
	978-1-944151-39-7	Money and Murder III	Fred Brown	$15.00	
	978-1-944151-49-2	Scandalous Ties	Jermaine "Ski" Buchanan	$15.00	
	978-1-944151-51-5	Scandalous Ties II	Jermaine "Ski" Buchanan	$15.00	
	978-1-944151-52-2	Scandalous Ties III	Jermaine "Ski" Buchanan	$15.00	
	978-1-944151-55-3	Scandalous Ties IV	Jermaine "Ski" Buchanan	$15.00	
	978-0-9799556-2-4	Courts in the Streets	Kevin Bullock	$15.00	
	978-0-9822515-5-3	Courts in the Streets II	Kevin Bullock	$15.00	
	978-1-944151-43-0	Courts in the Streets III	Kevin Bullock	$15.00	
		Total Books Ordered		Quantity	
				Subtotal	
SHIPPING/HANDLING (Via U.S. Priority Mail) $7.20 for 1st book, $2.00 for each additional book Institutional Check & Money Orders ONLY (No Personal Checks Accepted)				Shipping Total	
		Total		$	

www.ingramcontent.com/pod-product-compliance
Lightning Source LLC
Chambersburg PA
CBHW020632250626
47154CB00008B/2638
* 9 7 8 1 9 4 4 1 5 1 0 4 1 *